ROCKET SCIENCE

By K.M. Neuhold

DEDICATION

To the incredible and talented Z.B.Heller. I swear
I was channeling you during a few scenes in this
story. Your strength and resilience is an inspir-
ation and I love you to pieces.

CONTENTS

SYNOPSIS

Relationships aren't rocket science. If they were, I might stand a chance of figuring one out.

Elijah
Saying I've had a crush on my best friend's older brother, Pax, most of my life is like saying the big bang was just an explosion. It's true, but I'm not sure that quite captures the essence of its true enormity.

I know he's only hanging out with me because I'm new in town, and getting my PhD doesn't leave me with much time to make friends. And even if it did, my strength is mathematics, not friend-making. What I don't understand is why he kissed me...why he seems to want to keep kissing me. I don't think my advanced physics knowledge is going to help me figure this one out. But I think for once I'm okay with not knowing, as long as Pax and I don't know together.

Pax
He's still the awkward Nerdlet I remember...he's

also probably the cutest, most tempting man I've laid eyes on. I know I should keep my hands off him, but this thing between us is like a force of nature. I want to be his first everything. He says we're nothing more than atoms crashing into each other. I'm no scientist, but I don't think either of us are braced for the explosion.

**** Rocket Science is a stand-alone MM romance featuring an inexperienced nerd, a cocky player, and a satisfying HEA

COPYRIGHT

Rocket Science© 2019 by K.M.Neuhold

Cover by Natasha Snow
Editor: Editing By Rebecca

CHAPTER 1

Pax

Ice clinks against the sides of my glass as I lift it to my lips. My eyes slowly scan the bar, taking in all of my options and doing a quick mental calculation of exactly how much effort each man would take to get into my bed based on a number of factors I discovered and tested during my college years. Some of my friends told me I was wasting my genius on matters of my dick, but I honestly can't think of a better use for my brain than this.

I catch the eye of a twink a few feet away— petite, a little too petite for my taste if I'm being honest, although nothing the generous curve of his ass doesn't make up for. He holds eye contact as he rolls his straw between his teeth, assessing me the same way I was just assessing him. His gaze lingers on my arms, my dress shirt rolled up past my forearms, showing off the colorful ink normally hidden beneath.

I throw back the last of my drink and pre- pare to approach what seems to be a sure thing, when my phone buzzes in my pocket. I consider ignoring it since there's a good chance it's my boss, and he can suck my dick if he thinks I'm taking a call from him after nine on a Friday night.

But on the off chance that it's someone *other* than my jagoff of a boss, I reach into my pocket to check. My brother's name lights up the screen, and I try for a second to fathom why Theo would be calling me. Not that we don't get along, but most of our interactions are limited to birthday texts and catching up at the holidays, maybe tagging each other in the occasional meme on social media. For the life of me, I can't remember the last time we spoke on the phone, if ever.

My heart beats a little faster, worst case scenarios filling my mind as I hit the accept button and lift the phone to my ear.

"Is everything okay?" I ask immediately.

"Uh...yeah." He doesn't sound particularly sure about that, but since he doesn't seem to be panicking in any way, I assume everyone we know is alive and not in any sort of mortal peril.

"Good. What's up, bro?"

"I sort of have a favor to ask," he hedges, and my interest perks.

"Oh, yeah? Hit me."

"You remember Elijah?" he asks, and I chuckle, reaching for the fresh drink the bartender places in front of me.

"Of course, I remember little Einstein," I

9

answer, images of the knobby kneed, bespectacled nerd my brother called his best friend through most of his childhood fill my mind. With our age difference, I left for college when Theo was only ten, so I can't say I knew much about his life or his friends, but I always got a kick out of Einstein.

"He's not little; he's twenty-three."

I give a low whistle. "Where does the time go?" I ask rhetorically. "Please tell me he's still all knees and elbows with a head too big for the rest of his body?"

I swear I can hear my brother rolling his eyes through the phone. "Sure, why not," he responds, tone dripping with sarcasm.

"What's the favor?"

"He just moved out to Pasadena, he's in the PhD program at CalTech."

I whistle for a second time. "Damn, good for him."

"Yeah, the thing is…" he pauses and sighs, clearly weighing his words. I give him time, glancing over at my potential conquest again, only to find him hanging all over some other man. *C'est la vie.*

"What *is* the thing, T?" I prompt when I grow impatient.

"He's not the greatest socially. It was fine during undergrad because we were in New York together, but I'm worried that since he doesn't know anyone out there in California, he's going to become a hermit. He'll never go anywhere except for campus and his tiny little studio apartment, and he'll die of loneliness."

"Die of loneliness, huh?" I respond dryly. My brother always was a bit of a drama queen from what I could tell.

"Don't scoff. Social belonging is on Maslow's Hierarchy of Needs. Social interaction is important just like food and shelter."

"Well, at least we know the buttload of money you shelled out for that psychology degree was worth it."

"Pax, I'm being serious."

"Okay, what do you want me to do about it?" I ask with a sigh, leaning my weight against the bar, the desire to pick up some strange for the night slowly fading.

"I want you to hang out with him a little, just to get him out of his apartment. You don't have to be his babysitter forever, introduce him to some people so I'll know he isn't *completely* alone out there."

There's a hint of desperation in Theo's voice that keeps me from brushing him off completely. Spending my time with a gangly, socially awkward, nerd is *not* near the top of my list. But Theo's right, it's not like I need to become besties with the guy, we can meet up for drinks, maybe I can introduce him to a few acquaintances, no big deal.

"Fine, text me his number," I agree.

"Thank you, thank you, thank you. I owe you one, big time."

"I'm going to hold you to that," I tease.

We hang up, and my phone vibrates a few seconds later with a text from Theo with the phone number. I save it in my phone as Einstein and return my attention to the hunt.

Elijah

I pop a piece of popcorn into my mouth and let it melt on my tongue for a few seconds, soaking up the buttery, salty flavor before chewing and swallowing. I reach for another piece, careful not to knock any of my snack onto my stack of notes and textbooks open on the table. Page after page of calculations are spread out in front of me, and the last thing I need is to get them all covered in popcorn grease. I wipe my hand on my jeans and reach for my pencil to continue working.

A pleasant feeling of peace and pride settles over me as the equation starts to come together, the calculation for a satellite's orbit emerging. There's a reason numbers have always made more sense to me than people do. Numbers are simple: they always do what you expect them to do. It's what drew me to aerospace engineering, the ability to see a problem and find a solution using known mathematical principles of physics is amazing. Plus, *rockets*.

People, on the other hand, rarely do what I expect. They say things that are different than what they mean, they laugh and tease, they lie. People don't make sense the way physics and numbers do; they don't even try to.

I glance over at the model rocket on my dresser, squished in beside my bed, in the corner of the room. It was a present from my best friend, Theo, before I left New York. Theo doesn't make sense either, but I like him anyway. He's kind and funny, even if he always had a bad habit of forcing me to leave the house and be around other people I didn't like all that much.

A slightly tight, uncomfortable feeling settles in my chest that I'm sure is somehow associated with thinking about my very best friend thousands of miles away. It was inevitable that we would have to part ways, I knew that early on, but I never expected to miss him when it happened. I suppose over the years, he wormed his way further under my skin than I expected.

As if summoned by my thoughts, my phone lights up from its place on top of my fluid mechanics textbook, Theo's name across the screen.

"Hello," I answer.

"Hey!" he responds with so much enthusiasm I have to pull my phone from my ear to prevent being deafened. I switch to speaker phone and set it back on top of my textbook. "How'd the move go? Did you get all settled in? Are you ready to start your classes next week?"

"Move went smoothly. My place is roughly the size of a shoebox so I'm pretty much tripping over all my stuff. But I have a table to study at and a bed to sleep on, so that's all I really need. And, yes, I'm very excited for classes to start. I've already begun reading the textbooks, and I'm unwinding with a few calculations tonight."

Theo snorts a laugh on the other end of the phone, and I feel myself bristle a little. I know sitting at home on a Friday night calculating lift, thrust, and drag isn't most people's idea of a fun night, but for me it is. Some people do sudoku, some like to do craft projects, I like to solve equations. I don't see what's so wrong with that.

"Have you explored the neighborhood at all? Checked out any of the local bars or anything?"

"Why would I do that?" I ask, my attention slipping from the conversation as it veers in a direction I'm less than interested in entertaining.

"You're so close to campus, I bet if you went to a bar, you'd run into other students there," Theo suggests, his tone holding the implication that something like what he's describing would somehow be a desirable outcome.

"Then what?" I already know the answer. I'd make small talk, pretend to be interested in where they lived before they came to California and how much they can't stand their roommates, or whatever it is college students like to talk about. They'd pretend to be interested too, asking me all sorts of questions I have no desire to answer before politely making up an excuse to walk away so they could laugh with their friends about me.

"Then you'd make a friend," he says with a hint of sadness in his voice, like it's paining him to have to explain this to me.

"I already have a friend," I point out.

"We have an entire country between us," he argues.

"That doesn't diminish our friendship." Emotional bonds are strange that way. Unlike physical forces, they are in no way impacted by the distance between the two objects—or people as the case may be. It's fascinating when you think about it.

Theo sighs, and I hear a rustling on his end of the phone; I assume he's making himself more comfortable.

"I called Pax," he says, and my heart finds its way into my throat, my stomach fluttering violently at the mere mention of Theo's older brother, Paxton.

For most of my childhood, he'd been little more than Theo's largely absent older brother. Being eight years older than us, he barely noticed our existence and vice versa. When he went off to college, it hardly registered. That is until the summer when I was thirteen.

Most of my peers had begun putting all their energy into fawning over members of the opposite sex. Boys gathered to whisper about which girls wore the shortest skirts and whose bra they'd like to get under, and the girls giggled and flirted right back. Theo was the exception, confessing to me in a whisper one weekend during a sleepover that he thought he might like boys. I was the outlier, it seemed, finding no interest in members of either sex at the time. I was far more consumed with ways to improve the design of the model rockets I'd gotten at the hobby shop so they could go higher, fly farther.

Then it happened, Pax came home from college for the summer.

The first time I *really* noticed him he was mowing the lawn...shirtless. I'd stood dumbfounded on the side of the house, my pants becoming tight as I stared at the way his muscles bunched and moved, each trickle of sweat sliding down his bare torso. I remember smiling with relief, glad to finally have an answer to where my interest lay. Maybe I was simply a slightly late bloomer, or maybe it was that the scrawny, pimply boys my own age couldn't hope to compete with the perfection of a twenty-one-year-old college boy.

I watched him a lot that summer, stoking my growing crush with furtive glances and late-night fantasies about what it would be like if he were to notice me in the same way I was noticing him. When he came out to his parents near the end of the summer, my crush reached its peak. I was sure one day I would know what it felt like to touch Pax, kiss him, be *noticed* by him.

But then he left for his final semester of college, moving to California for work after graduation, and I hadn't seen him since.

"Why'd you call your brother?" I ask, shaking myself out of my ill-timed walk down memory lane.

"I gave him your number, told him you two should hang out since you live in the same city."

"You what?" I nearly shriek, standing from my chair so quickly that it topples backward and lands with a loud bang against the floor. My glasses start to fog up from the heat of my face, so I take them off to wipe them on my shirt. "God, Theo that's so embarrassing. Why would you do that?"

I can only imagine what Pax must be thinking, his younger brother calling and begging him to take pity on his pathetic, socially awkward best friend. Is there a hole somewhere I can crawl into and die? Because that would be absolute perfection right about now.

"Because I'm worried about you," Theo says. "You have a lot in common."

K.M. Neuhold

"Like what?" I challenge.

"Um...he's really smart."

"He's a salesman," I point out. Not that there's anything wrong with being a salesman, but it clearly demonstrates that Theo's confident, stupidly handsome older brother continues to have the kind of social skills I could only ever dream of.

"So? I'm sure there's a ton you two could talk about. If he calls, go out with him for *one* drink. If it's horrible and awkward, I won't mention it again."

"It's already horrible and awkward," I complain, finally righting my chair and sinking back into it. "I don't think I can even answer if he calls, it'll be too embarrassing. I can feel myself turning all red and squirmy just thinking about it," I confess with a shudder.

"Pax is a nice guy. I bet you two would have fun hanging out," he insists. "Please give it a chance, for me?"

I swear I can hear Theo's puppy dog eyes through the phone. If it wasn't for the fact that I owe him immensely for every time he stood up to a bully for me in high school and all the times he made me feel less alone, I would outright refuse. But I can't.

"Fine," I agree with a sigh. "*If* he even calls."

"He'll call," he says confidently. "Now, I've gotta run, enjoy your equations."

"Always," I assure him.

CHAPTER 2

Pax

I drop my briefcase on the floor as soon as I step through the front door of my apartment, kicking off my shoes carelessly and collapsing onto my overstuffed couch with a groan. It feels damn good to be home after a week traveling, selling security software to every tech company I can manage to score a meeting with. There's a certain thrill in selling, but at the end of a long week, my own apartment feels like heaven.

I loved this place the minute I laid eyes on it with its open concept, the spacious kitchen giving way to the living room, the exposed brick walls, the floor to ceiling windows in the bedroom. And, it's more than enough space for a hopeless bachelor like me.

A week has passed since my brother called and babysitting his Nerdlet friend has been the furthest thing on my mind. But it's a Friday night, which means after a much-needed shower and nap, my dick is going to lead me to the nearest bar to find someone bury myself inside and let all the stress of the week melt away. If I'm going out anyway, I might as well kill two birds with one stone: invite Einstein out for one drink and then send him on his way so I can enjoy the rest of my night.

I pull out my phone and type out a quick text.

Pax: Let's grab a drink. Meet me at Twisted Cherry downtown at 9

A response doesn't come immediately, so I heave myself up off the couch and make my way to the bathroom to take a shower, desperate to get the gritty feeling of travel off my skin.

By the time I get out of the shower, my phone is blinking with an unread message. I take my time drying off with a towel and wrapping it around my waist before picking my phone up off the sink ledge and checking the message.

Einstein: I'm sorry, but I'm fairly certain you have the wrong number.

I snort a laugh and shake my head and then hold my phone up to snap a picture of myself. My hair is wet and without my shirt on, the colorful tattoos covering my chest and arms are on full display. I wonder for a second if the kid will even recognize or remember me. It's been years since we've crossed paths. I send the picture, and it shows as being seen immediately, the little dots bounce indicating he's typing something, then they disappear, a few moments later they appear again, but I get tired of waiting for a reply, so I decide to get started on that nap I planned in the meantime.

I unwrap the towel from around my waist and hang it on the back of the bathroom door, then make a beeline for my bedroom and crawl between my cool, soft sheets. Before I can close my eyes, my phone vibrates with another text.

Einstein: Paxton, hi

I smile, an odd sort of affection filling my chest for the little Nerdlet. *That's* what took him so long to type and send?

Pax: Hi
Einstein: I'm sure Theo made me sound like I'm record breaking levels of pathetic, but I assure you, you don't need to take pity on me. I appreciate the invite, but you don't have to do this. I'll tell him we hung out and had a great time, that way he'll leave you alone.

That *would* be the easier option, but for some reason, I find myself slightly intrigued to see what the grown-up Nerdlet is like. Call it a bad case of curiosity.

Pax: No can do. A promise is a promise.
Pax: One drink

Again, in spite of the messages showing as read, he doesn't respond right away. It's an odd situation for me to be lying naked in my bed, staring at my phone, waiting for a message, and not have it be sexting. My dick could not be less interested in this situation, and yet, strangely, I continue to hold my phone and wait to see if Einstein is going to agree to meet up or not.

When a new text finally comes through, I scramble to open it.

Einstein: Fine. See you at 9.

A triumphant smirk settles on my lips, and I finally set my phone back down, pulling a pillow against my chest and settling into sleep.

*****

Twisted Cherry is crowded, but I manage to spot an unoccupied high-top table and snag it while I wait for Einstein to show. My eyes scan the crowd reflexively, even though right now I'm more curious to see the Nerdlet than to find a piece of ass. Images of him from all those years ago fill my mind and make me smile. He always seemed to be lugging around a bag full of textbooks that weighed more than he did, thick-rimmed glasses in place and curly hair that was *never* in place. I wonder if he still wears the t-shirts with the science puns on them or if he still keeps his inhaler on a string around his neck to keep from losing it.

I chuckle to myself at the thought and wave down the nearest waiter for a drink and then return to letting my attention wander. My gaze catches on a man as he wanders into the bar. He's not my usual type, but damn if he isn't pretty. His dark hair hangs in wild curls, flopping down over his forehead, his features are sharp, but his lips look full and soft, and I have no doubt they'd feel like heaven wrapped around my cock. He's wearing a pair of jeans, a black t-shirt, and a light-colored blazer that might look out of place in a bar on anyone else, but somehow looks absolutely perfect on him.

I have a hard time tearing my eyes off him, my dick growing hard in the confines of my jeans as I stare shamelessly, and he looks around the bar with a somewhat lost expression. He turns his head slightly, and our eyes meet, and a shy, awkward smile forms on his lips. My cock gets even harder as I return the smile, thoughts of the Nerdlet I'm here to meet fleeing my mind in favor of calculating the best method of seducing such a sweet little treat.

"Paxton?" he asks, and my heart sinks.

"Fuck me," I mutter, reaching for my drink.

Elijah

I draw up short, my stomach twisting with nerves as Pax takes a long gulp from his glass, his Adam's apple bobbing as he swallows. If I had any notion that he'd somehow become less attractive over the years, the photo he sent me earlier put that idea to rest. I nearly swallowed my tongue when the image popped up on my screen of my adolescent obsession clearly fresh out of the shower, possibly completely nude. The tattoos were a newer addition, and while I can't say tattoos are something I would generally classify as attractive, they certainly looked good on Pax.

I thought he recognized me when our eyes met, he'd smiled and seemed happy about my approach. But, after his angry utterance, I'm not so sure. I hang a few feet away from the table, waiting to see what he'll say next. Perhaps he changed his mind about getting together. Did I miss a text calling the whole thing off? My hand itches to reach for my phone to check, but my nerves are strung so tight all I can do is stand there like a deer in the headlights and wait.

"You grew up good, Einstein. I didn't recognize you at first," he says once he sets his glass down, a friendly smile on his lips now. He's so much like how I remembered him, blue eyes full of humor like there's an inside joke only he's privy to. Oddly, it doesn't feel like he's laughing *at* me, more like he's laughing with me, like I'm somehow in on the joke even though I haven't heard it. He drags his hand through his dark hair, which is longer on top and buzzed short on the sides. It looks nice on him.

"Really?" I look down at myself, wondering what could possibly look different about me. Sure, I dress a little differently now, but aside from that, I'm certain I look like I always have.

He chuckles, and the sound is rich and warm, sending a small shiver through me.

"Let's get you a drink," he suggests, flagging down a waiter and using his foot to push the nearest chair in my direction, an invitation to sit down, I would assume.

I wait a few seconds, assessing the situation before deciding that *yes, this is in fact an invitation to sit down.* I slip into the chair and fold my hands on the table in front of me, more acutely aware of them than I usually am. Hands are an odd thing, so useful and yet perpetually in the way.

"What can I get for you?" the waiter asks, and my mind goes completely blank. I've never been much of a drinker, and when I do drink, I typically always ordered whatever Theo was having. I glance at Pax's glass and then back at the waiter.

"I'll have what he's having."

"Sure thing, be back in a minute, sweetie."

The bar is loud, almost too loud to hear

myself think, but there's an awkward kind of silence that settles between Pax and myself. It occurs to me that although I've known him most of my life, the two of us have never had a direct conversation. My brain scrambles for something to say, panic setting in. This is exactly why socializing is agony. The only reason I managed a friendship with Theo early on was that he had a knack for filling silences like these.

"So...um..." I shift in my seat, tracing the grains of wood on the table with my index finger.

"I have to say, I'm a little disappointed you traded in your science pun t-shirts for a more adult wardrobe," he says with a hint of amusement, and my face flames.

I can't believe he remembers the t-shirts I used to wear. And now it definitely feels like he's laughing *at* me.

"Please don't make fun of me." The words surprise me as they fall out of my mouth firmly, even if they are hardly above a whisper. "I know this is a pity hangout, but don't be cruel."

His forehead crinkles, his eyebrows drawing together.

"I wasn't making fun of you," he says. "I really did like the t-shirts, they were funny."

"Oh." I'm not sure how it's possible but my face gets even hotter.

"So, tell me about yourself, Einstein. You're clearly not the little Nerdlet I remember."

It's the second time he's called me Einstein. I remember the nickname from when we were younger, and I can't believe he remembered it, but it also leaves me wondering if he remembers my actual name or not. If I wasn't already so embarrassed, I might ask.

"There's not much to tell." I shrug. "I'm in the PhD program for aerospace engineering at CalTech, which I think you already know. That's about it."

"There's no way that's it," he disagrees. "What about hobbies, boyfriends, deep seated insecurities you're dying to share over a drink even though we both know it's way too much information too quickly?"

"Um, no to all three." The waiter returns with my drink, saving me from any follow up questions. I reach for the glass and lift it to my lips, sputtering as soon as the first sip hits the back of my throat.

Pax chuckles again, and I consider turning tail and running before I can embarrass myself further, but unfortunately that would be equally as humiliating. He waves the waiter over again, and I give a sheepish smile.

"Can we add some Coke to this whiskey, help it go down a little easier," Pax requests, handing my glass back over and shooting me a wink.

"Sure thing," the waiter says, taking the

glass and disappearing into the crowd again.

"Oh my god, he's probably going to spit in my drink for causing him trouble," I lament.

"A little spit never killed anyone," he reasons, and my mouth falls open. "I'm kidding. I'm a regular here, I promise he won't spit in your drink."

The waiter returns quickly with my doctored drink, and it turns out the soda *does* help the whiskey go down a lot smoother.

*****

I'm not sure how long we've been at the bar or how many drinks I've had but my brain feels fuzzy and loose, my tongue seeming to have a mind of its own.

"And here I thought you were smart all these years," I tease, watching the way Pax's face lights with amusement, his formerly neat hair now hanging a bit disheveled over his forehead, his cheeks slightly pink, I'm assuming from the alcohol.

"I *am* smart," he counters. "I graduated top of my class with a degree in engineering, just because I decided to pursue the sales side of things does *not* mean I'm not smart."

"If you were smart, you'd know that there's *no way* the Millennium Falcon could do a Kessel Run in under twelve parsecs. It has one of the least aerodynamic designs I've ever seen."

"Not aerodynamic?" he repeats in disbelief. "Have you ever seen a frisbee? They're plenty aerodynamic."

"A frisbee is not a spaceship, different things need to be considered," I argue.

"You're right, considering that the space-crafts in *Star Wars* are capable of lightspeed travel, I'd say that aerodynamics aren't even what's really in question. What you want to consider is photodynamics."

My mouth falls open as I find myself at a legitimate loss for words.

"Furthermore," Pax goes on, pausing to drain his latest drink. "If you look into *Star Wars* lore, a parsec is a unit of distance, not a unit of time, so one can assume Han was just talking out of his ass to sound like a hotshot, rather than listing actual specs for the Millennium Falcon."

"Wow," I murmur, still dumbfounded. "Alcohol clearly makes me stupid, and also, you're a total *nerd*," I tease, letting the surprise infiltrate my voice. "I mean, I knew you were smart, but you're a nerd."

"Shut up," Pax says with a chuckle.

"Does anyone else know, or are you completely in the closet?" I ask with mock innocence.

"I'm not a nerd; *Star Wars* is completely mainstream," he argues.

"Yes but knowing that a parsec is a measure of distance rather than time is *not* mainstream."

"Are you hungry?" he asks, deflecting rather than acknowledging my statement.

My stomach rumbles at the question.

"Starving," I say, standing up and wobbling on my feet. I grab for the table to steady myself and nearly take the whole thing down. "Dang, I am *way* too drunk."

Pax stands up gracefully. He's had at *least* as much as I have, but he's clearly better at holding his liquor than I am. He slings an arm over my shoulders and pulls me against him. My whole body heats at the contact.

"There's a killer burrito place across the street, let's go."

Pax

Whoever's idea it was to open a late-night burrito place smack dab in the middle of all the bars on the street is clearly a genius. I have no clue if the burritos are even any good since I've never tasted one sober, but I do know they hit the spot after a fuckload of alcohol.

"What's good here?" Einstein asks, looking up at the menu and swaying on his feet.

"Grab a seat, I'll get the food."

He wobbles to the nearest table without protest, and I order our food. I keep an eye on him while I wait for our burritos to be up, and it becomes clear I'm not the only one who thinks he's pretty damn cute. A table of guys who came from Twisted Cherry eye him and exchange

31

what I'm sure are lewd comments. I wonder which of the guys at the table, if any, are his type. Theo *did* ask me to help him socialize after all, so the ponderance is relevant, or so I tell myself.

Once our food is up, I grab the trays and carry them over to the table.

"Here you go, Nerdlet," I say, setting his down in front of him. He frowns up at me.

"Do you remember my name?" he asks suspiciously.

"Elijah," I purr, the alcohol in my system unleashing my flirty side with full force. But I refuse to acknowledge the way his name rolls off my tongue or how cute he is when his cheeks pink.

"Oh," he says a little shyly, reaching for his food and digging in without another word.

"This was fun; we should do it again," I say as I dig into my own burrito. The words are a surprise even to me, but as soon as they're out, I realize they're true. Once he loosened up a little, this was a fun night, even if I didn't end up picking anyone up to take home.

"Get drunk and eat burritos?" he asks.

"It doesn't have to be this *exact* thing, but the general concept—hang out, drinks, food, building a bond that may someday be considered friendship."

And there's that blush again.

"Yeah, that sounds good," he agrees, keeping his eyes on his food while a shy smile forms

on his lips.
    "Good."

CHAPTER 3

Elijah

It feels like there's a jackhammer inside my skull doing its level best to break out. I groan, rolling over in my bed and swallowing back the wave of nausea that washes over me. Bits and pieces of last night flicker back into my memory—drinks, *so many drinks*, Pax and I laughing and talking, burritos...

The thought of the burritos has my stomach revolting in a violent fashion. I throw back my blankets and bolt for the bathroom with one hand over my mouth. Falling to my knees in front of the toilet, I wince as the cold tile touches my skin, and I lose the battle against my stomach, emptying its contents into the toilet. Once I'm sure I've puked up everything I've eaten in the last week, I rinse out my mouth and pathetically shuffle back to my bed, grabbing my phone off the nightstand as I go.

Elijah: I'm never drinking again
Theo: Lol, omg did you actually leave your apartment???
Elijah: Your brother texted me and said we'd

have ONE drink. The man is Satan. He got me drunk and took advantage of me.

Theo: What?!?!?!

Elijah: Not like THAT. Calm down. He kept buying me drinks is all I mean. We actually had an ok time. At least I think we did. I had a good time, and I'm sure Paxton was humoring me and was glad to finally be rid of me when he poured me into an Uber sometime around two in the morning.

Theo: Jeez, don't scare me like that again. I thought I was going to have to buy a plane ticket to come out there and fuck my brother up.

Theo: And I'm sure he had fun too. You're a fun person, E, you just need to let loose a little.

Elijah: Oh, I was plenty loose last night.

I wince at the memory of calling Pax an idiot. He didn't seem too upset by it though, and he *did* say he wanted to hang out again, although I'm sure he was just being polite.

I pull my blankets up to my chin and close my eyes again, not interested in anything other than more sleep and whatever will stop the pounding in my head. My phone vibrates again on the bed next to me, and I reach for it, expecting another text from Theo, most likely including some kind of sexual innuendo I'll only partially understand. My heart jumps into my throat when I see who it's actually from.

> **Pax:** How are you feeling this morning? I got the impression you aren't normally much of a lush.
>
> **Elijah:** Pretty sure I'm dying
>
> **Pax:** That's unfortunate. Try some aspirin and a glass of water, it may turn out to be a miracle cure ;)
>
> **Elijah:** Ok, I'll do that once I can move without wanting to puke again
>
> **Pax:** Where do you live?
>
> **Elijah:** Near campus, why?
>
> **Pax:** Because I'm planning to stalk you, and it'll be a lot easier if I get your address

My stomach gives a little flip at his teasing, my fingers hovering over the keys, my mind desperately trying to come up with something witty to say in return. I'm not delusional. I know my stupid little teenage crush isn't going to come to anything, but it *would* be nice to have a friend out here in California. If I could somehow become the kind of person who knows the right things to say, who's funny and confident, maybe Pax really would want to be my friend. But no matter how hard I wrack my aching brain, I can't come up with anything funny to say in return, and the longer I wait the more awkward a reply will be. Instead, I just text him my address. Why he wants it, I can't begin to guess.

It shows that the message was read, but he doesn't respond, so after a few minutes I close my eyes and let myself fall back asleep.

The sound of my buzzer jolts me out of sleep sometime later. I search my sleep fuzzy brain, trying to remember if I ordered something from Amazon because I can't imagine anyone other than UPS ringing my bell. Maybe someone else in the building forgot their key and randomly pressed my buzzer hoping I'd let them in. My head falls back onto my pillow, and I sigh tiredly, trying to decide if it's worth it to get up to see who's at the door. The buzzer sounds again, and I throw my blankets back and reluctantly get out of bed. I'm sure my hair is sticking up in every possible direction, and I'm not wearing anything aside from my t-shirt from last night and my boxers, but if it *is* UPS, I can just buzz them in and let them leave whatever it is I forgot that I ordered outside my apartment door until I can put some pants on.

I shuffle to the intercom and press the button.

"Who is it?" I ask.

"Delivery," a falsetto voice answers, and I scrunch my brow.

"What kind of delivery?"

"You ordered a...*companion*." The last word is said in a breathy, suggestive kind of way that has my face heating, even though there's no one here to have heard it besides me.

"I, uh, I think you have the wrong apartment," I stammer out.

"Isn't this Elijah Cummings?" They ask, putting emphasis on my last name in a way that makes it sound untoward. Not like I didn't get enough jokes about it in middle and high school, I don't need a prostitute turning it into some sort of suggestive dirty talk.

"Yes, but I didn't...I'm not...Um..." I don't want to be *rude*, clearly this person's wires got crossed. Maybe there's another Elijah Cummings in the building, although even without sitting down to calculate the odds of that, I'd bet they're astronomical.

"Einstein, I'm fucking with you," Pax says, dropping the falsetto.

"Oh," I say, my breath whooshing out with relief. I only have a few seconds of relief before I realize that Pax is at my apartment and I'm half naked. "Um, give me a second," I tell him through the intercom, shaking off my hangover and bolting over to my dresser to grab some pants to pull on. I rake my fingers through my hair in an attempt to tame some of the curls and then hit the button to unlock the outside door.

A few moments later, there's a knock at my door, and Pax actually *is* here, in my apartment, holding a takeout bag and smiling like he isn't so hungover he wants to die.

Pax

Elijah looks like death warmed over. His hair looks like he stuck his finger in a light socket, and there's a little bit of crusty drool on the corner of his mouth. He glares at me as I hold out my offering with a smirk.

"How do you look so chipper right now?" he asks suspiciously. "If you have a secret hangover cure, you have to tell me."

"Lucky you, that's exactly why I'm here," I say, shooting him a playful wink as I rattle the bag in my outstretched fist. He eyes it with curiosity but doesn't make a move to take it, so I sigh and slip past him into his place.

It reminds me of the apartment my friend, Hudson, and I shared right after I moved to California—tiny, cramped, peeling paint.

"It was in my budget," Elijah says defensively, his shoulders slumped as he watches me take in his place.

"We all lived in shitty places while we were in college; there's no shame in it." I reach into my pocket and pull out a couple of aspirin I stashed there earlier. "Here, take these." Elijah looks at the pills in my hand like I'm offering him heroin, and I chuckle. "It's aspirin, take them."

After a few more seconds of hesitation, he reaches for the pills and pops them into his mouth.

"Thank you."

"You're welcome. I'm not sure why you're

so suspicious of me. I came bearing breakfast."
I hold the bag up again, and this time he looks
a little more interested. "No better hangover
cure than a couple of greasy bacon and egg sandwiches."

"I can't decide if that sounds delicious or
if it makes me want to puke," he admits, leading
me over to the small table near the kitchen. It's
covered in textbooks and scattered notebook
paper, which he quickly sweeps into a stack, setting them all onto the floor so we have space.

"You'll feel better once you eat it, trust
me."

We sit down and dig into our breakfast.
I can feel Elijah's gaze flicker to me every few
moments, but he doesn't say anything while he
picks at his sandwich, carefully chewing each
bite.

"Why'd you bring this stuff over?" he asks
once he finishes his food, sitting back in his
chair, his eyes fixed on the table as he draws
random shapes on the surface with his index finger. No, not random shapes, numbers...an equation? It's hard to tell but I'd rather focus on that
than on the question he asked. I'd like to say it
was because I knew it's what Theo would want
me to do, to look out for his best friend. But
Theo wasn't on my mind this morning when I
shoved a couple of aspirin into my pocket and
beelined for the nearest fast food drive thru. I'm
not entirely sure what was on my mind other

than the goofy, drunk smile that had graced Elijah's lips last night while we argued about *Star Wars* and physics.

"Just being a good Samaritan," I answer with a shrug. "Did the semester already start?" I ask, jerking my chin toward his textbooks in a blatant attempt to change the subject.

"It starts Monday."

"In that case, on Friday we'll have to celebrate your first week as a PhD student," I declare, and he turns a little green.

"No alcohol," he says with a grimace.

"All right, no alcohol," I agree, and then an idea strikes me. "You know what, I have the perfect idea for how we can celebrate."

"Oh?"

"There's a vintage arcade downtown. Technically, it's a bar too, but we don't have to drink. We can stick to soda while I kick your ass at *Pac-Man*."

Elijah snorts and rolls his eyes. "You are dreaming if you think you can beat me at *Pac-Man*."

I smirk at him. "I guess we'll find out Friday."

There's a spark of challenge in his eyes as he finally looks up at me, a small smile on his mouth as well. "I guess we will."

CHAPTER 4

Elijah

There are plenty of things I absolutely suck at—social interaction being the main one, obviously. But school? School is something I excel at. A deep sense of calm fills me as I set foot on campus for my first day of grad school. It's nothing like my first day of undergrad, dodging frat boys and art students drawing chalk murals on the sidewalks. If it hadn't been for Theo, I probably would've spent every second of the four years in the library or hiding in my dorm. I still did as much as possible, but he did drag me out to bars or campus events weekly.

A sad ache starts in my chest. I haven't had a first day of school without Theo at my side since elementary school. He took me under his wing the first day of fourth grade, claiming me as his badminton partner in gym after everyone else quickly paired off, leaving me feeling every bit of an outcast as I always seemed to be. I didn't know the first thing about having a friend, but Theo didn't seem to mind. We were inseparable after that for thirteen years. Now he's on the complete opposite side of the country.

I have the urge to call him and tell him how silly and nostalgic I feel starting a new school year without him here, but if I don't hurry, I'm going to be late for my first class.

I push the wistfulness aside and hurry to class. The classroom is extremely nice, clearly well-funded, with comfortable chairs and spacious desks, a state-of-the-art whiteboard at the front of the room. I've always been torn between grabbing a seat at the front of the room in order to get the best view without distractions and staying near the back where no one will notice me. I linger near the back for a moment, nerves battering my stomach as I weigh my options.

"I like your blazer," someone says and my face heats. Was it sarcastic? It's hard to tell. My stomach twists in knots, and I wrap my fingers tightly around the strap of my messenger bag filled with all my textbooks and notebooks. "There's an open seat here if you want it," he offers, and I finally look over in his direction.

He's not what I was expecting. He reminds me a bit of Theo with a petite build, blond hair styled into a small mohawk, and a friendly smile on his face. He's wearing a t-shirt with Bill Nye on it that says Science Rules. He looks like he's about sixteen, and I wonder for a minute if he's even in the right place.

He gestures to the empty seat beside him, and I hitch my bag higher on my shoulder and weave through a few chairs to get there.

43

"Hi, I'm Alex," he offers, holding his hand out. I wipe my sweaty palm against my jeans before reaching out to shake his hand.

"Elijah," I say, sliding into the open seat.

"I know what you're thinking," he says wisely, giving me a serious look. "And yes, I'm naturally this adorable."

A surprised laugh bubbles past my lips. Yup, he's basically Theo in a different body.

"Lucky you," I joke.

"Seriously though, I *am* only eighteen, I finished high school when I was fifteen and then got my undergrad done in three years, so here we are."

"Oh wow." So, he's a genius and apparently isn't lacking in social skills or self-confidence. I've heard of such unicorns but haven't seen one in the wild before now.

"Are you in the aerospace engineering PhD program?" he asks.

"Yeah, rockets," I answer, mentally smacking myself in the head. *Obviously rockets, dumbass.*

"Me too. I guess we'll be seeing a lot of each other over the next few years."

"Yeah," I agree, nodding my head and forcing a smile. He smiles back for a few seconds, and I wonder if there's more I should say. Should I suggest we hang out sometime? Or is he just making polite conversation?

I'm saved from having to figure it out by

the professor starting class, everyone else falling silent in order to take copious notes.

When class ends, Alex suggests we walk to our next one together. Apparently, the program is small enough that anyone in the major has the same schedule. I guess we *will* be seeing a lot of each other over the next few years.

As we walk, he points out guys he thinks are cute and chatters away about the bars and clubs he's already checked out in the area before switching seamlessly to analyzing some of the information we learned about fluid dynamics and what he'd already read ahead about in the textbook. The latter is obviously a conversation I'm much more skilled at holding, and I decide I can definitely see becoming friends with Alex. Look at that, I've officially doubled my record number of friends. Theo would be so proud.

Pax

As soon as I step into my hotel room, I shed my suit jacket and unbutton the top few buttons on my shirt. Kicking my shoes off, I groan and flex my toes.

The hotel room is painfully generic. It could be any hotel in any city. I would know, I've been to most of them. When I took this job, I was excited about the idea of travel. I spent most of my life living in the Midwest, going to the University of Illinois for college. The fact that this position was based in California was enough to entice me, but the thought of getting to fly different places nearly every week, talk to people running multi-billion-dollar companies, I wanted it badly.

I do love it as much as I thought I would. But that doesn't make these bland, boring hotel rooms any more bearable. Sometimes it helps to head to the nearest bar or jump on a hookup app and find some company. Usually, I've got a pretty man face down, ass up on the bed, which makes noticing the décor less of a priority. But not tonight. Tonight I am alone.

I consider the option for several seconds, pulling out my phone and flopping down on the bed. But for some reason, it holds less appeal than it usually does. Which is strange because half the excitement of weekly travel is different hookups in every city.

Instead, I order room service and turn on the TV to browse through the movie options. When I see the new *Star Wars* movie listed, I click on it and pick up my phone, a smile forming involuntarily on my lips.

Pax: Lightsabers don't make sense at all
Einstein: True, they do not. I think the plasma beam theory is probably the closest to realistic, but even that has some major issues
Pax: What about contained laser photons?

Einstein: It would be so hot it would literally incinerate anyone near it
Pax: Hmm, someone's going to have to call George Lucas and ask what he was thinking
Einstein: Solid plan
Pax: Wow, was that sarcasm? I wasn't sure you had it in you, Nerdlet.
Einstein: Was this just a pretext to tease me?

With anyone else I might take that as a joke too, but there was something about the shyness in Elijah's eyes when we hung out that tells me he's just as insecure as that message sounds.

Pax: Not at all, Nerdlet. Just bored.
Einstein: Oh
Pax: What are you up to?

I add a few pillows behind my head to get comfortable, the opening lines of *The Last Jedi* playing in the background while I watch the little dots bounce on the screen, letting me know Elijah is typing.

Einstein: Homework
Pax: It's the first week of school, how can you have homework?
Einstein: You realize this is a PhD program, not middle school, right?
Pax: Still. Better you than me.

Einstein: You're parents said you were good at school. They always bragged about you having a 4.0 GPA at U of I

My fingers hover over the screen of my phone, his words striking me. He isn't like the guys I'm used to chatting with, he actually knows me. A strange feeling skitters along my skin, and I can't decide if it's a pleasant one or not. There's a certain kind of safety in being able to shape others' opinions of me, being able to create the exact persona I want them to see. Elijah knowing me like he does leaves me feeling oddly exposed.

Pax: I didn't hate school, but I'm more than glad to be on to the rest of my life
Einstein: I don't even know what I'll do when I'm finished with school. I would rather it never end because real life is daunting
Pax: You'll be some big, fancy rocket scientist working for NASA
Einstein: Shut up, that's terrifying

I chuckle to myself and type a response, the bland emptiness of the room fading into the background.

CHAPTER 5

Elijah

All week I half expect to find out Pax was just messing with me about wanting to hang out. It would make a lot more sense for this to turn out to be some kind of elaborate prank than for him to actually want to be my friend.

After the night he texted me about *Star Wars*, our text conversations became more frequent. All week he sent me funny memes—science cat seems to be his favorite, and I'll admit, I enjoy the puns as well. But even the frequent messages didn't put my nerves at ease. There has to be some sort of trick to this, doesn't there? Why would someone like Pax want to spend any more time with me than he has to?

The thought strikes me that maybe Theo is still putting him up to it. My stomach twists, and a grimace tugs my lips down.

"Big plans tonight?" Alex asks, pulling me out of my broody thoughts.

"Hmm?"

"It's Friday night, you must have something fun going on."

"Oh, no," I answer automatically before

remembering I *do* have plans. "Actually, I'm hanging out with a f-someone tonight. We're going to some arcade or something."

"Is he hot?"

My face heats, and I turn my attention to my open textbook, hoping I can avoid answering. Of course, Paxton is hot, but it's not like it matters. There are tons of hot people in the world; I don't see what difference it makes. And why does Alex care anyway?

"I might not even go. I have a lot of reading to do for class," I say vaguely.

"Oh, so he's ridiculously hot," Alex says with an air of knowing. "It's always the ridiculously hot ones that make us all nervous and stupid."

"*Everyone* makes me nervous," I mutter, and he laughs, giving me a pat on the shoulder.

"I don't make you nervous," he points out, his hand lingering on my shoulder for a few seconds, leaving me wondering if he's trying to hit on me or if he's just extremely friendly. I squirm under his touch, and he chuckles again.

"The only person who doesn't make me nervous is my best friend, Theo," I inform him.

"Why doesn't Theo make you nervous?"

I shrug, hoping the motion will dislodge his hand, but it remains firmly in place. "He never laughs at me, and he always tells me how he really feels about things, so I never have to guess. He always stood up for me when kids picked on me in middle school and high school."

"Wow, he sounds like a real Prince Charming," Alex says with a tone I don't quite understand.

"He's just Theo."

"Huh."

"I don't know what that means," I grumble with irritation. This is what I mean, people don't make sense and it's frustrating.

"It doesn't mean anything. I was just thinking about what you were saying," he explains simply. "For what it's worth, I think you should go."

I give him a curious look, and he stifles what sounds like another laugh.

"Tonight, you should go hang out with the hottie. Even if you're in love with Theo, it doesn't mean you can't hang out with other guys until the two of you find your way to each other."

"What?" I sputter, my eyebrows jumping up as I try to figure out his words. "If I'm in love with *Theo*?"

"Well, yeah, it kind of sounds like—"

"No," I cut him off, shaking my head and smiling at the absurdity. "Theo's my friend, that's it."

"So, what's the problem with the hottie?"

"There's no problem, I just hate socializing, and it's been a long week so I'm not sure I'm up for a whole night of worrying that I'm saying or doing something stupid." The confession surprises me. It's the kind of thing I'd normally only confide in Theo, but Alex broke down my defenses with his ridiculous theory.

"You know what I do when I'm afraid of saying something stupid?"

"What?" I ask.

"I purposefully say something *really* stupid right away to get it out of the way. If he laughs it off with me, then I know we can have a fun date, and I'm able to relax. If he's weird about it, I make an excuse and get the hell out of there."

My mouth falls open as I consider the sheer brazenness of that tactic. I push my glasses up my nose as they start to slip. He *purposefully* says something stupid knowing that someone else will hear it?

"That's...wow, if I wasn't sure I'd burst into flames with embarrassment, I'd totally try that."

"Embrace the embarrassment," he advises. "It's never killed anyone."

"That you know of," I point out. "Thanks for the advice though."

"No problem." He finally releases my shoulder, and I sigh with relief.

Pax

I lean against the rough brick exterior of the arcade, waiting for Elijah. I thumb through my phone, looking back over our text exchange from the past week and smile. Little by little, he's come out of his shell, and I'm curious to see what he'll be like tonight. Without any alcohol in the mix and without a phone screen as a buffer, will he be back to shy, blushing Elijah, or will he be the Elijah who calls me an idiot while we argue?

He comes into view, headed down the street with his hands shoved in his pockets, his shoulders hunched like he's trying to make himself small so no one else on the street notices him. And it seems to be working as people shuffle past him without a second glance. How anyone could miss him is beyond me. He doesn't look so different from last week, wearing another stylish blazer over a plain t-shirt and a pair of jeans. His hair is combed, unlike the morning I brought him breakfast, and I find myself missing the wildness of his curls when he was clearly just out of bed. *I bet he looks incredible after a hard fuck.* The thought hits me like a punch in the gut, stealing my breath for a few seconds before Elijah's eyes meet mine, and I force myself to smile at him and pretend excitement isn't stirring between my legs.

"Hey," he greets nervously.

"Hey, Einstein, good to see you."

He blinks at me with a hint of surprise in his eyes like he can't believe it's actually good to see him. My heart breaks a little that he feels that way, and I suddenly understand my brother's fussing over his friend. There's something about Elijah that makes you want to shield him from the big, bad world.

"How was your flight?" he asks as I shepherd him into the arcade.

"Eh." I shrug. I typically fly twice a week so there's not usually much to note unless there's some sort of major crisis. "There was a hot flight attendant who flirted with me most of the flight."

"Only you," he mutters, shaking his head, and I laugh.

"Aw, jealous, little Nerdlet? Would it help if I told you it was a woman, and I wasn't the least bit interested?"

"I wasn't jealous," he argues, but the tight set of his shoulders eases, but I decide to leave it alone.

"Ready to get your ass kicked at *Pac-Man*?" I ask, nodding toward the nearest machine.

"You wish," he counters, darting for the game.

Elijah does in fact kick my ass at *Pac-Man*, but I get him on *Space Invaders* so I'm okay with it.

"So, no boyfriend. What's the deal with that? Too busy being a genius or what?" I ask conversationally when we take a break from the games and sit down to order some greasy bar food.

The blush that creeps into Elijah's cheeks

makes the question one hundred percent worth it.

"I don't...um..." He fiddles with the buttons on his blazer, looking anywhere except at me.

"Did I put my foot in my mouth? Theo said you were gay, was he not telling me the whole story? Are you ace, and I'm being totally obtuse right now or something?"

He finally looks at me and gives a sharp shake of his head. "No, I'm not ace or aro or anything; I just don't date."

"Why not?"

Elijah huffs out a humorless laugh. "People don't make any sense. Like, there's all these things you're supposed to say or do to let someone know you're interested, but nobody ever told *me* what those things were. And people lie, not just with their words but with their smiles and their eyes. They pretend to like you just so they can laugh about it behind your back or copy your homework."

My heart breaks for him, his words hitting closer to home than I'd like to admit to myself.

"So, you've *never*...uh...dated?" I ask as delicately as I can manage. I'm sure it's none of my business, but I find myself curious anyway.

"I just said I didn't," he answers, looking at me like I'm an idiot. Then, understanding dawns in his eyes. "You're talking about sex now, right?"

I snort a laugh into my glass of soda I just lifted to my lips to drink. Reaching for my napkin, I mop it across my mouth. "Yes, I meant sex."

"I'm a virgin," he says matter of factly. "There's nothing wrong with being a virgin."

"Didn't say there was."

"Oh please, I bet you're the kind of guy who has a different beautiful man in his bed every weekend," he accuses, a bite in his tone that I can almost mistake for jealousy.

"That's not very polite. If I don't judge you for *not* having sex, it's not exactly fair for you to judge me for what goes on in my bedroom."

He blushes again, a deeper pink this time that's endlessly satisfying.

"You're right, that's not fair of me," he agrees.

When he doesn't go on, I lift my soda to my lips again and take a drink, now that I'm not at risk of snorting it through my nose.

"I could help you, if you wanted," I offer casually.

"What do you mean?" That suspicious look is back in his eyes.

I shrug, not actually sure what I meant when the offer forced its way out of my mouth, bypassing my brain entirely. "If you wanted lessons on how to flirt or how to spot guys who are receptive to being picked up."

"I'm certain I'm a lost cause," he says. "I wouldn't want to waste your time."

"Waste my time? You think I consider hanging out at gay bars on Friday nights and flirting with cute men a waste of time?"

Elijah's face falls a little, and his shoulders sag. "I'm sorry I was keeping you from that. I told you I didn't need a pity friendship. Go, flirt, don't worry about me."

"I'm not *worried* about you, and this isn't pity," I argue. "I like hanging out with you, and I think it would be fun to go scope out guys together, but if you're not interested, we can leave it at that."

The waitress drops off our food, and we both dig in, leaving the conversation alone for now. I'd love to see Elijah let loose a little and find the confidence I'm sure is under his shy exterior, but I'm not going to force him.

We play games for a few more hours, each of us winning a few. Elijah grows more relaxed as time wears on until he's the same laid back, sarcastic man I hung out with last weekend, just minus all the alcohol.

A yawn forces its way out of me, and I check the time, surprised to see we managed to nearly shut down the arcade.

"Oh wow, it's late," he says. "I should probably head home." He bites his bottom lip, looking unsure of himself. If this was some random at a bar, I'd guess from his body language that he was trying to work up the courage to invite me back to his place. But this is *Elijah*.

He orders an Uber, and I wait with him. When the car pulls up to the curb, he gives me a shy smile and opens the back door to get in, stopping before he pulls the door all the way closed, he gives me that look full of nervousness and a spark of interest again. I bet it's the exact same look he'd have if I had him pinned beneath me, naked and desperate. My cock shifts against my leg, hardening as my thoughts take a dive into the gutter without my permission.

"I'll do it," he says, and for a crazy second I think he can read my thoughts and is agreeing to the filthy things running through my mind.

"Do what?" I ask, my voice coming out huskier than intended.

"The flirting. You can teach me…if you really want, I mean."

I blink and shake away the fog of debauchery clouding my brain. "Oh, yeah, of course."

A slow smile spreads over his pretty pink lips, and he finally pulls the door closed behind him, giving me a little wave through the window before the car pulls away, leaving me horny and confused on a street corner in the middle of the night.

CHAPTER 6

Elijah

Pax: What are you wearing?

I read the text and then glance down at my clothes, wondering if there's a certain dress code I'm not aware of for the bar he's dragging me out to tonight to apparently teach me how to flirt. I'm absolutely positive I'm a lost cause, but if he wants to waste his time, I can play along for one night, I suppose.

> **Elijah:** Pretty much the same thing I always wear—jeans, a red V-neck t-shirt, and a black blazer. Is that ok for this bar? I don't really have much else. I guess I could skip the blazer?
> **Pax:** No
> **Pax:** I meant What are you wearing? ;)

I look down at myself again, trying to decipher his meaning. Is he asking about the brands of my clothes? Because seriously who knows that?

Elijah: I don't understand

Pax: I'm flirting, Einstein

Elijah: OH!

Pax: Ok, let's try this one more time...What are you wearing? ;)

Elijah: Um...I'm not sure what to say. If I'm not wearing something sexually suggestive do I lie? Or should I strip down to my boxers and then I wouldn't be lying when I say I'm in my underwear?

Elijah: But also, is what I already told you ok for the bar tonight? I could figure something else out if it's not.

Pax: You're killing me, Nerdlet lol

Elijah: Sorry, I told you I was hopeless

Pax: You're not hopeless, but we may need to work with your unique personality to develop a flirting style all your own

Elijah: *sigh* I'm hopeless

Pax: What you're wearing sounds fine, I'll pick you up in half an hour

Elijah: You don't have to. I can take an Uber

Pax: It's no trouble. I'll see you soon

I can't actually believe I agreed to this. After our night at the arcade, we texted all week again, and it was clear that Pax was taking this seriously. It seemed he spent all week trying to decide on exactly the right bar, texting me suggestions for opening lines when approaching someone I'm interested in, and detailing the kind of body language I should watch for, including YouTube videos for reference.

I almost told him to forget about the whole thing. It's too much, too stressful, too pointless. I don't need to be some smooth-talking Lothario, picking up guys in bars. Maybe I'll die a virgin; I'm fine with that.

That's a lie. I'm absolutely *not* fine with it, but it seems like a less painful alternative to actually trying to find someone to do those things with.

*****

It's a different bar than we met at last time, but it's more or less the same—music that's just slightly too loud, lots of men in various states of intoxication flirting with each other, dim lighting. As far as I can tell, this is the general motif for all bars, plus or minus the gay parts.

"Want a drink?" Pax asks, his hand coming to rest on my lower back as he guides me through the crowd. I allow myself a single second of indulgence, pressing into his touch before moving forward.

"All right, but only *one* drink," I agree, still sick at the memory of the hangover I had the last time.

"You got it," he agrees with a hint of amusement. "Grab that table, and I'll hit the bar to get us some drinks."

I snag the table he pointed out and slide onto the tall stool. While I wait, I let my attention wander around the bar. The way everyone interacts and moves around each other is like an organized sort of chaos that fascinates me. I imagine them as elements, some of them crashing into each other to create chemical reactions or, if they're lucky, to become something totally new and different than they were before.

A man approaches the table with a wolfish grin, and I offer a polite smile in return.

"Hi," he says as soon as he reaches me.

"Um, hi. Sorry, did you want this table? I'm waiting for a friend, but I'm sure we can share if you want."

His eyebrows scrunch together for a second, and then he lets out a loud laugh. I recoil at the sound, my stomach tightening. *I said something stupid, and now he's laughing at me.* It's not like when I was confused about Pax's text earlier; this man isn't laughing with me like Pax was.

"I don't give a fuck about the table, sweetheart."

"Oh." I'm not sure what to say. Why is he here? Then it hits me. "*Oh.*"

"The person you waiting for, is he your boyfriend?" The man leans over the table, his eyes devouring me shamelessly. He's not bad looking, all things considered, but something about him makes me feel dirty just having his eyes on me. I shudder at the thought of *more* than his eyes on me.

"Um...yes," I lie, and his face falls.

"Bummer. If that changes, find me later." He gives me a wink and then saunters away. I sag with relief, letting out a long breath.

"What happened? He seemed interested." Pax appears in an instant as if materializing out of thin air. I startle and then glare at him.

"Were you watching me?"

He shrugs and sets my drink down in front of me, sliding onto the stool opposite me.

"I was on my way back, and I noticed him approaching you. I didn't want to cock block."

"He wasn't my type," I answer, taking a sip of my drink and making a surprised noise when the sweet concoction hits my tongue. I have no clue what it is, but it tastes a lot better than whatever I got last time.

"What *is* your type then? I need details if I'm going to help you scope."

"I don't know." I drag the pad of my index finger along the rim of the glass.

"Come on, Einstein, you must know what turns your crank. Don't be shy," he encourages.

My eyes drag over Pax in a way I hope is inconspicuous. When I first started crushing on him what feels like a lifetime ago, he wasn't the man he is today. Back then, his preferred wardrobe seemed to be shirtless with grungy cargo pants that were in desperate need of being tossed out. He didn't have any tattoos, his hair was a little longer and generally messier, and he didn't have any facial hair. The man in front of me might as well be a different person with his dress shirts, sleeves always rolled up to show off the colorful tattoos on his forearms, his hair stylishly coiffed, just a hint of stubble on his cheeks and chin. Which is my type? It's hard to say because both versions of him light a fire in me like no one else has.

"I think it's more about their personality than how they look," I say.

"That's going to be harder to spot from across the room, but not impossible. What are we looking for, brainiacs like you or what?"

I give a sharp shake of my head, tongue darting out to wet my lips. "Confident, funny, maybe a little bit arrogant."

"You're making it too easy, Einstein," he says with a smirk, lifting his own drink to his lips and taking a sip. "Guys like that are easy to spot and even easier to flirt with."

"They are?"

"Sure. With those types of men all it really takes is letting them know you're interested in their attention, and they'll be more than happy to give it."

I take another sip of my drink and give a shaky nod. My tongue darts out, gathering a few sweet droplets as I shift nervously in my seat.

"So, um...how...how would I let someone

like that know I'm...um...interested?" My heart is beating so hard I can barely get the question out, but Pax seems completely unaware, scanning the bar absently.

"Compliment him, look at him like he's the only man you can see in the whole bar, and a little casual touching goes a long way. You don't need to go over the top, but a brush of the arm can really create a spark he won't be able to ignore."

Pax

I keep my eyes scanning the bar, hoping that if I don't look at Elijah, he won't be able to see the irritation on my face. I'm not even sure what's getting under my skin. Maybe it's the fact that I haven't gotten laid in weeks. That would irritate anyone.

Warm fingers brush against my forearm, and I finally let my attention focus back on Elijah, which is exactly where it wants to be. That shy look is back in his eyes, his cheeks pink, whether from the alcohol or from nerves, I can't tell. He traces the lines of the dragon on my forearm, his touch sparking along my skin like flint on kindling.

"I like your tattoos."

"Yeah? I wouldn't have pegged you for a tattoo guy," I say, unable to tear my gaze away from Elijah as he looks up at me through his long eyelashes, his curly hair hanging over his forehead.

"I'm not sure I am, but they're nice on you."

Something burns in the pit of my stomach. It's similar to the kind of lust I have for the randoms I take home, but somehow burning deeper inside of me, hotter and more desperately than I've ever felt before. I clear my throat and pull my arm back, away from his touch.

"I guess I shouldn't be surprised that you're a fast learner," I joke, smiling to hide the way my heart is beating too fast, my cock hard as steel in my jeans. "Now let's find you a real target to practice on."

His face falls as he pulls his own hand back onto his side of the table.

"I think I changed my mind," he says, pushing his glasses up his nose.

"What?"

"I don't think I want to flirt with random guys. Not tonight anyway," he confesses. "I'll just get an Uber home, and you can stay and have fun. I've been cramping your style the past few weeks anyway; I'm sure you'd like me out of your hair." He gives a quiet, self-deprecating laugh.

"If you're not up for a night out, why don't we head back to your place and order a pizza, watch a movie, or something," I suggest.

"You don't want to do that." He shakes his head, standing up and shoving his hands into his pockets. "You said this is your idea of a fun Friday night." He nods toward the throngs of people filling the bar.

"Nah, I'm not into it tonight." I push my half-finished drink away and stand up. "Let's go."

CHAPTER 7

Elijah

Butterflies assault my stomach as Pax drives us back to my apartment. I made such an idiot out of myself trying to flirt with him at the bar. I don't know why he didn't just put me out of my misery and let me get a ride home on my own.

"You really don't have to come up," I assure him as he pulls into a spot in front of my building. "I'm sure spending a Friday night in a tiny apartment watching movies isn't your idea of a good time."

He cuts a glance in my direction, eyeing me for several seconds before responding.

"What if I want to come up?" he challenges.

"That's fine. I just don't want you to think you *have* to." That's what this is all about after all, isn't it? He's only here because Theo made me sound like the most pathetic loser on the planet, in desperate need of a friend.

"Einstein, do I seem like the type of guy who does *anything* he doesn't want to do?"

"No, I guess not," I concede.

He nods and turns off the car, getting out without another word.

As soon as we're inside my apartment, he makes himself at home, grabbing my remote and opening the Netflix app on the TV. I watch him in awe for a few seconds, wondering what it must be like to feel so comfortable in your own skin, to go through the world with confidence and ease. I bet it's wonderful. If I had that, I probably wouldn't want some awkward dork trying to flirt with me either.

"Do you want me to order a pizza?" I ask, not feeling particularly hungry but happy to have an objective to focus on.

"In a minute, come here first." He pats the couch cushion next to him, and I hesitate. Am I about to get some kind of speech about how he only sees me as a friend? It's not necessary; I already know it. Of course, Pax isn't into me, it wouldn't make any sense to think otherwise. The attempt at flirting was a lapse in judgment on my part, temporary insanity.

I sit down anyway, bracing myself for an awkward end to our fragile, short lived friendship.

Pax doesn't say anything right away, simply looking at me with an intensity in his eyes that I can't interpret. Is he mad? He must be, that's the only thing that explains it.

"I'm so—"

But I don't get the chance to get the

69

apology out, to tell him I never should have flirted with him and beg him to forget it ever happened. For reasons I doubt I could decipher if I spent the rest of my life contemplating them, he cuts me off with his lips against mine.

My breath catches, and my brain short circuits. Did I give him a sign I didn't know I was giving? And if so, what was it so I can be sure to do it again.

Regardless of how or why it happened, Pax's mouth is moving against mine, warm and firm, commanding the kiss, consuming me as his fingers slip into my hair, using the grip to tilt my head and deepen the kiss, his tongue slipping past my lips. I couldn't begin to guess how many times I imagined what it would be like to have Pax's mouth on mine, but every fantasy pales in comparison to the reality of the hungry way his lips move, the feeling of his teeth as they scrape across my bottom lip, his body pressed against mine as his tongue dips into my mouth, making me shiver with need.

He swallows my moans, my fingers gripping tightly to the front of his shirt, my lips desperately trying to keep up while my heart beats wildly against my ribcage.

Pax's free hand slips under my shirt, his fingers ghosting along my stomach, leaving goosebumps in their wake. I want to take my shirt off to feel his skin against mine, but I'm afraid to break the moment. I have no idea what's happening or where this is going; all I can do is hang on for the ride and pray that whatever insanity has Pax's hands and mouth on me doesn't pass before I have a chance to see how this plays out.

Wanting to feel more of his body weight against me, I lean back, pulling him along with me until he's blanketing me, pressing me into the small couch. I can taste the ghost of the strong drink he had at the bar, and when both his hands find their way under my shirt, caressing my skin, I'm sure I'm going to lose my mind, completely drunk on him.

"Can we..." I gasp against his mouth, barely able to hear my own words over my pulse thundering in my ears.

"Anything," he murmurs, dragging his lips along my jaw, the rough stubble on his cheeks abrading my skin. "Tell me and I'll give it to you."

His words wash over me and lick at my skin like fire. His teeth scrape along the juncture of my throat, and I moan, pressing my hard, aching erection against his through our jeans.

"Bed," I manage to gasp, protesting immediately when he responds to my request by climbing off of me. I reach for him with a whimper, catching his shirt in my fist and attempting to drag him back.

"Come here," he encourages, laying his hand over mine, twisted around the fabric of his shirt, the other looping around my waist to pull me up off the couch. His lips crash into mine again as soon as my feet are under me, and I cling to him like he's the port in a storm.

I don't even realize we're moving until the back of my legs hit the bed.

"You're in the driver's seat here, Einstein. Tell me what you want," Pax says, his voice thick and deep, his eyes wild. His neat hair hangs mussed over his forehead, the first few buttons on his shirt undone, likely when I grabbed him, exposing his tattooed chest, rising and falling with each rapid breath.

"I don't know," I gasp, fingers fumbling to undo the rest of the buttons on his shirt as he kisses along my throat, nibbling and sucking. "I don't...um...*oh god*." I moan as he bites down on my collar bone, my cock pulsing, trapped in my jeans.

"Do you just want to kiss a little?" he suggests.

"No, more." I push his shirt off his shoulders and watch as it falls to the floor at his feet. He's nothing but miles of colorful skin stretched over muscle, and I think it may be making me even stupider than the alcohol did before. All I can do is stare at him and try to think of a million different ways I could touch him. But I don't have time for a million ways, this might be the only chance I have, so I start by leaning forward and pressing a kiss to the center of his chest, taking a deep breath, filling myself with the scent of his woodsy soap and sweaty skin.

The dusting of hair on his chest tickles my face, and all I can think about is how it would feel to be skin to skin, with nothing else between us.

Pax's hands cup my face, his lips finding mine again as I struggle to get my blazer off, dropping it to the floor as soon as I'm free, and then grabbing the hem of my shirt to pull it over my head. Our lips part for a fraction of a second but it's physically painful. Dramatic, I know, but now that I've tasted Pax's mouth, I'm not sure how I'll survive without it when this is all over and reality leaks back in.

The feeling of bare skin against bare skin is even better than I thought it would be, heat sparking at every point of contact between us until I'm sure we're seconds from going up in flames.

"You didn't answer my question, Elijah," he murmurs against my mouth. The sound of my name on his lips sends a thrill through me, my cock jerking and my balls tingling as a moan forces its way from me.

"What question?" I ask, unable to remember anything other than the feeling of his body grinding against mine.

"Tell me where the line is so I don't cross it."

"I don't know," I answer again, vaguely

recalling already having had this conversation. "Not...um...not *everything*."

"Got it," he assures me. "Pants on or off?" he checks, his fingers grazing along the waistline of my jeans, making me tremble.

"Off," I answer instantly. *Oh my god, I'm going to see Paxton without pants on. If this is a dream, please, please, please don't let me wake up before I get to see his dick.*

My fingers are shaking almost too much to get the button of his pants undone, but by some miracle of god or science, or possibly sheer luck, I manage it. As soon as the zipper is down, the bulge of his erection strains forward, stretching the front of his underwear to the point that I can see the entire outline through the strained material.

My mouth goes dry, my heart in my throat. I am in so far over my head right now I don't think I could find the surface if I tried, and I'm not sure I *want* to try. No, what I want is to run my finger along the outline of his cock and memorize the way every hard ridge feels. I want to drop to my knees and take him in my mouth. The fact that I don't have the first clue how to please him that way barely crosses my mind. I want to figure it out with my mouth so full of his cock that I can hardly breathe. Actually, forget breathing all together, I'm almost certain that's how I'd like to die, choking to death on Pax's cock.

And then my pants and boxers are around my ankles, and Pax is touching me.

"Oh my god, oh my god, oh my god," I pant, my entire body nearly convulsing at the feeling of his warm, firm grasp around my erection, stroking me slowly from root to tip. My eyes roll back, and my toes curl into the carpet, my balls constricting. "Wait, oh my god, wait," I manage to gasp before it's too late.

"Was that too much?" he asks, concern filling his tone. I shake my head quickly, pulling at every ounce of courage I can find and using it to shove his underwear down too.

His cock is *huge*, slapping against his stomach with a resounding *thwack* once it's freed from its prison. My eyes go wide, and I try to calculate the proportions, absolutely positive that there's no way that thing would fit inside any part of me. There must be a way, right? He can't have the largest dick in all of existence, and people find ways to make it work all the time.

I reach out slowly, pressing my palm against his shaft and wrapping my fingers around it. I gasp at the impossible heat radiating off of him, the smooth feeling of his silky skin in my hand, sheathing the hard steel of his arousal.

"I don't know what I want because I don't think I know everything there *is*. All I know is that I want to feel you against me, I want you on top of me and all around me, I want to see what it's like when you fall apart from pleasure." If they weren't coming out of my own mouth, I wouldn't believe the words were my own. There's a desperate, lustful edge to them...I sound *sexy*.

"You have no fucking clue how irresistible you are, do you?"

The question confuses me. I'm sure it's rhetorical, but it doesn't make sense either. Before I can puzzle over it for too long, Pax pushes me onto the bed and climbs on top of me.

He fits himself between my spread legs, his hot, hard cock lining up against mine, pressing against me in the most mind-melting way. His mouth devours mine, and he starts to thrust against me.

My moan is muffled by his tongue, pleasure like I've never felt before rushing through me as his cock grinds against mine. I can't begin to count all the places our bodies are connected, but I swear every single one of them is an erogenous zone. I can't breathe, I can't think, I can't do anything but feel.

With every thrust against me, Pax grunts around my tongue, and I'm certain I'll never hear a sexier sound in my entire life. My skin grows damp with a mixture of sweat and precum, his and mine. His arms rest on either side of my head, caging me in, as if I'd ever want to get away. I drag my fingers through his hair, over his chest, along his back, desperate to feel and memorize every inch of him before this is over.

His thrusts are hard and fast, and it's too easy to imagine he's inside of me instead of on top of me. What would it feel like to have him stretching and filling me? It's not something I've thought much about, figuring maybe I wasn't so into the idea of penetration at all. But I'm thinking about it now. Oh boy am I thinking about it. My hole clenches and aches at the idea, my whole body on edge as he ruts against me.

"You're so sexy," he murmurs against my lips, his words catching me off guard. "So sexy, so perfect, so fucking good," he groans, moving faster, pressing me harder into the bed until I can't fight it any longer. I cry out, a scorching wave of pleasure washing over me as my cock pulses cum onto my stomach. He doesn't stop thrusting, the feeling of his cock dragging against mine prolonging my orgasm until I'm sure I'll never be the same again. In French, the word for orgasm is *le petite mort*, the little death. That's exactly what this feels like. I've died and been reborn in an instant.

Pax lets out a loud groan, and his hot seed joins mine in covering my stomach and my softening cock.

Pax

"Wow." Elijah breathes out the word as if he's just seen the face of God, a blissed-out smile on his lips, his skin flushed pink, sweat clinging to him along with our release, smeared on his stomach in the most obscenely sexy way I've ever seen.

I bite back a groan as the reality of the situation crashes down around me.

What the fuck did I just do?

His eyelids flutter closed as soon as I climb off of him, desperately fighting against the panic rising in my chest, squeezing my lungs until I can hardly breathe.

Can I claim temporary insanity? Because that's what that felt like. It was like an out of body experience. I can't pinpoint the moment I even decided to kiss him; it was like someone else was in control of my body, some lusty beast who'd been watching Elijah through my eyes for weeks now and refused to be contained any longer.

I need to get out of here.

"Stay?" he asks in a voice so quiet I almost don't hear him. It's only a single word but it carries the weight of the world with it. I can't stay. I *don't* stay. I've never *wanted* to stay, and I'm not sure I would know how even if I did. But the vulnerability in his tone—even with his eyes closed, I can feel him bracing for rejection, and I can't bring myself to do it.

"Sure thing, Einstein. Why don't we get cleaned up first though," I suggest.

"Nuh-uh," he mumbles, shaking his head back and forth against the pillow and yawning.

"You don't want to go to sleep covered

in..." My breath catches as I take in the sight of him for a second time, so perfectly debauched. "Like *that*."

"I want to," he argues, his voice low and a little throatier than usual, his fingers trailing from the middle of his chest down to the mess on his stomach. He drags them through our release, rubbing it into his skin, and my cock twitches, attempting to get hard again at the unintentionally erotic display.

I decide not to argue, pulling back the blankets and slipping beneath them. Elijah reaches over and turns off the light, and within seconds his breathing is deep and even with sleep.

Rolling onto my back, I stare up at the ceiling, the only light from a streetlamp just outside. My stomach twists itself in knots that I'm not sure I have any hope of ever unraveling. Sweat cools on my skin, my heart pounding too hard, whether from the sex or from my racing thoughts, I can't say. It's probably a bit of both.

My brother asked me to look out for his best friend, and I end up humping him like a horny dog. *Classic fucking Paxton.* I grit my teeth and clench my eyes closed, wishing like hell I was someone else, someone who didn't let his dick make decisions that inevitably blew up in his face.

I turn my head to look at Elijah, fast asleep beside me, lying on top of the bedsheets, gloriously naked in the moonlight. His pale skin looks almost luminescent in the darkness, and the urge to reach out and touch him again is almost too much to bear. I clench my hands into fists at my sides, determined not to give in to the urge.

I always wondered if Theo had a thing for his best friend, considering how much he's always talked about Elijah, how the two of them were joined at the hip since middle school, how protective of him he's always been.

Fucking fuck.

I scrub my hands over my face wishing like hell for a way to set this whole situation right, to make it like it never happened. Except...

Elijah gives a snuffly snore, and my heart cracks open a fraction.

No.

I steel myself against the longing threatening to wash over me. I fucked up, and I need to set this right.

Pushing the covers back as slowly and quietly as I can, I climb out of bed. It takes me a few minutes to locate all of my clothes in the darkness, but eventually I manage it, dressing as silently as possible and watching for any signs of Elijah waking up.

I breathe a sigh of relief when I make it out of his apartment and into the hallway without him stirring. I sag against his door and close my eyes, refusing to acknowledge the ache in my chest or the part of my brain that's still gloating about being the first person to taste Elijah's lips, to hear the sounds he made just before he came, to feel him writhing in my arms.

I swallow around the lump in my throat and force myself away from the door, refusing to be drowned in the hurricane of emotions swirling through me—guilt, longing, despair...

I manage to push myself away from the door and walk away from the apartment where Elijah is sound asleep, still covered in my cum.

CHAPTER 8

Elijah

The sound of my phone buzzing drags me from a very deep and pleasant sleep. I grumble and rub my hands over my eyes, dislodging the crust that formed while I slept. My eyes aren't the only thing that's crusty, the skin on my stomach itches from the dried ejaculate, the rest of my body sticky with sweat.

I glance over at the other side of the bed to find it empty, the sheets disheveled, and the pillow clearly used, but no sign of the person who was there when I passed out. My stomach flutters and clenches at the same time, unable to decide if I'm horribly embarrassed by what happened or thrilled by it. Maybe if I wasn't waking up alone it would be easier to determine the answer.

My phone buzzes again, and I reach for it to see Pax's name across the screen. A twinge of hope takes up residence in my chest. Maybe he had somewhere to be early, a meeting with a client perhaps. He's calling to apologize for leaving while I was asleep.

"Hello?" I answer, my voice a little rough

with sleep.

"Einstein," Pax says cheerfully. "Hope I didn't wake you?"

"As a matter of fact—"

"I had a hankering for pancakes this morning, I thought you might want to meet me for breakfast."

Pancakes? That's the reason he slipped out of bed while I was still asleep? Clearly, I don't know much about the etiquette of...what we did, but this feels like somewhat of a bad sign.

"About last night—" I start, but he cuts me off again.

"Pancakes. Starving. Hurry." He hangs up before I can respond, and moments later, my phone vibrates again, this time with a text that contains the address of the restaurant where he wants me to meet him.

There's an unsettled feeling in my stomach as I climb out of bed and make my way to the bathroom for a quick shower. I don't care if he said to hurry; I'm not going to show up covered in sweat and...other things.

I step under the hot spray of the shower and reach for my bar of soap, memories of last night running through my mind as I scrub away the evidence. Pax was acting like nothing even happened. I suppose I should take a cue from him and behave that way as well.

Then, a horrible thought hits me. What if nothing *did* happen? Is it possible I had some sort of psychotic break and imagined the whole thing?

I close my eyes and try to recall the feeling of Pax's flesh under my fingertips, the taste of his tongue in my mouth, the feeling of his body pinning me down and thrusting against me. Surely that can't all have been a figment of my imagination. Even a very realistic wet dream can't be *that* good.

On the other hand...would he really go so far as to *pretend* nothing happened?

I finish my shower and dry myself off and then stand naked beside my bed, phone in hand, trying to decide if I should text him to beg off of breakfast or not. Another text comes through, a photo of a table with a cup of coffee on it and the caption *hurry up*.

With a groan, I toss my phone on the bed and get dressed, pulling on a pair of dark jeans, a white t-shirt, and my favorite striped blazer. With a quick glance at my hopelessly curly hair, already drying, sticking up in every possible direction, I pocket my phone again and head out.

My knee bounces as buildings whiz by outside the window of the Uber. Luckily, I didn't get a particularly chatty driver this morning. Five stars. Although, maybe a little distraction wouldn't hurt.

I keep playing the scenario over and over in my head, trying to figure out *why* Pax would leave while I was asleep and then call me to meet him for breakfast. It's a puzzle I can't seem to solve. It's the kind of thing Theo would probably have some excellent insight into, but I can't exactly tell him what happened...can I? No, probably not.

I sigh and lean back against the seat, tilting my head back a little so I can see the sky, slightly overcast this morning, overhead. I imagine the rocket or satellites I'll design one day, too far above the Earth to be easily seen. I could design something one day that could take people to places we've hardly dreamed of reaching. Surely, that's more important than whether or not Paxton likes me or not. It's a childish thought, at best, and yet it won't stop plaguing me.

When we pull up outside the restaurant, I almost tell the driver to take me home instead. I'm not sure I can face him after what happened. I don't have the first clue how to act or what to say. Then, I remember Alex giving me the advice of saying something stupid right away to take the pressure off, and I nearly laugh out loud. I think I reached the embarrassment equivalent of maximum density last night so how much worse can it really be this morning?

With a deep breath, I get out of the car and head into the restaurant.

Pax

I'm in uncharted territory, and I've never

been one to enjoy navigating the unknown. I'm used to having a handle on any situation, especially those involving sex. It's simple, find a hot guy who's interested in a little fun, have said fun, part ways, and move on with life. Einstein fucked everything up. Or maybe I'm the one who fucked everything up. I'm not entirely sure at this point.

I meant to go home after I slipped out of his bed last night, but I found myself driving around aimlessly until the sun came up, chasing my thoughts around hopelessly. And I have no more clarity or peace this morning than I did last night.

We had fun, and normally that should be enough. That's how it works, it's the only way I know how to make it work. And that's exactly the problem. He's a friend. I didn't expect it to happen, but he is. I enjoy spending time with him, and sex will only complicate things. Especially sex that good. The symphony of his moans plays on a loop in my mind, images of his body writhing under mine, the beautiful flush in his cheeks as his pleasure mounted.

I slam my coffee cup down, hot liquid sloshing over the sides and onto the table.

"Wake up on the wrong side of the bed?" a shy voice asks, and I turn my head to see Einstein standing awkwardly a few feet away, shifting from foot to foot, his cheeks pink just like in my memories.

Woke up in the wrong bed, I want to say... or maybe the problem is it felt like the right bed, and it shouldn't have. Instead, I give him a charming smile and gesture to the seat across from me.

"Took you long enough; I've been wasting away waiting for you."

"I had to shower," he explains, and another unbidden image of last night forces its way into my mind—Elijah's stomach smeared with our combined release, remnants of his orgasm clinging to the tip of his cock, sweat beaded on his forehead and matting down his wild hair.

He slides into the chair and reaches for the upside-down coffee mug in front of him, turning it over and filling it from the carafe, letting the strained silence sit heavy between us while he doctors it and stirs.

When he finally looks up, the uncertainty in his eyes cuts me deep and makes me feel like the world's biggest prick. He deserves an explanation for my behavior, but I can't seem to find the words. Instead, an even older memory surfaces in my mind.

"Do you remember when you were like twelve and you nearly blew up my parent's garage?"

"Theo bet me I couldn't build a rocket from scratch that would go higher than the store-bought ones," he explains, a small smile dancing on his lips.

"That's always been the image of you in my mind ever since, running inside with Theo on your tail, your face covered in soot, your hair slightly singed. Do you remember what you said?"

His head ticks to one side, and I can see the wheels turning in his eyes as he drags a finger absently along the rim of his coffee mug. "I said that I'd made a miscalculation." As the words leave his lips, understanding dawns in his expression. "Miscalculations can happen, and sometimes they blow up in your face," he concludes, and I nod.

He takes a deep breath and then lifts his coffee to his lips.

"Elijah," I say, and his name feels strange on my lips. It must sound strange too because he looks up at me sharply. "I called you as a favor to my brother, and I know you accepted the invitation to hang out for the same reason. But I feel like we've actually become friends. We *are* friends, right?"

He gives me a half smile, his tense shoulders sagging, and he nods, making his curls bounce against his forehead.

"We're friends," he agrees.

"Good." Some of the tightness that's lived in my chest since last night eases.

Our breakfast comes, and the subject moves on to less dangerous topics—his classes, where I'm scheduled to travel next week...but unlike every other time we've hung out, we don't make plans for next weekend. Maybe it'll do me some good to have a small amount of space to get my head on straight and forget last night. I haven't seen my other friends in weeks; they're probably starting to wonder if I've fallen off the face of the Earth.

I pay for breakfast, and the uncertainty of the moment hangs between us. I nearly ask what he's doing the rest of the day, suggest somewhere fun we can go to enjoy the beautiful late summer day, but I don't. Without a word I watch him get into an Uber and drive away, the knots in my stomach pulling tighter as he goes.

CHAPTER 9

Elijah

This week has been miserable. I had a feeling Pax was trying to let me down easy with all that *we're friends* stuff, but I didn't expect that he'd stop texting altogether. I didn't realize how much I'd come to enjoy his daily texts over the past few weeks until they completely stopped.

I pick up my phone and open to the last text he sent me, the address to the pancake place. A ghost of his words from that night echo in my mind, his raspy voice telling me I'm sexy and worthy of his attention, if only for a few minutes. I try to cling to them, even as they turn to dust in my hands.

I've considered texting him a million times this week. I missed his random musings, his complaints about clients, the pictures of random things in random cities. But I didn't know what I would say, so I never texted.

I sigh, pushing my phone away with a heavy feeling in my chest. It's almost a crushing weight, keeping me from drawing in a full breath. I wonder if this is what Theo is always talking about when he says how terrible loneliness is. I've never minded being on my own so much—I've preferred it even, but whatever *this* is, I don't like it all that much. I rub my hand over the center of my chest and slump back in my chair, papers full of equations spread out on the table in front of me, doing nothing to distract me.

My phone lights up, and my heart leaps into my throat. Could it be Pax finally calling to tell me how busy he's been all week, too busy to text, but I'd better hurry up and get dressed because he's coming over to drag me out somewhere *fun*. My hands shake as I reach for the phone, my breath whooshing out of my lungs when I see it's actually a call from Theo.

"Hello?"

"Hey, sugar plum, how's it going?" Theo greets cheerfully. The familiar sound of his voice manages to soothe me and somehow increase the weight on my chest.

"It's going," I answer without enthusiasm.

"It's a Friday night, please tell me you have plans."

I frown even though he can't see me. "Why is it your Friday night plans are allowed to consist of sitting at home worrying about me, but *I'm* expected to go out and live out the plot of some wacky teen movie where I get into all kinds of shenanigans and end up kissing my crush at the end of the night?"

Theo cackles out a laugh, and I reluctantly

smile at the warmth of the sound. "For your information, *I* have a date. But calling my bestie to check in always takes precedence."

The mention of a date causes my mood to sink even lower, making me thoroughly annoyed with myself. I've never cared about dating before. I'm perfectly content on my own. So why did one night with Paxton ruin me?

"What's wrong?" my best friend asks, suddenly serious.

"I didn't even say anything, what makes you think something is wrong?"

"I know you, E."

I sigh, shifting the phone to my other ear and getting more comfortable, leaning forward and putting my elbows on the table.

"There was this guy..." I confess, and Theo gasps dramatically.

"Are you serious? Tell me everything."

"There's nothing to tell." At least nothing I want to tell Theo. It seems weird to tell him what happened with his brother, and it's not like it amounted to anything more than a *miscalculation*, so it's not much of a lie.

"Elijah Morgan Cummings if you don't tell me about this guy right now, I'm getting on the next plane to California," he threatens, and I snort a laugh.

"I'm starting to think you're nothing but talk," I joke.

"I'm serious, I want to hear about this guy.

How'd you meet him? What's he like? Is he nice, I hope?"

"Honestly, it's nothing. We fooled around, and then the next day he told me we're better as friends more or less."

"Ugh," he groans. "I *hate* that line. Just man up and tell me you aren't interested."

A reluctant smile tilts my lips. I don't know how he does it, but Theo always makes everything better.

"I'm sure it was my fault. It was my first... well, anything, so I probably kiss like a fish and god knows what else. He probably couldn't wait to leave when it was over and then did his best to let me down gently so I wouldn't feel bad," I lament, my face heating with embarrassment at the admission.

"Stop it," he commands. "I hate this guy."

"You don't even know him." Now I'm even more glad I didn't mention that it's his brother. The last thing I want would be to create tension between them.

"I know he made you feel bad about yourself. And I know you must really like him, which makes the fact that he treated you that way even worse."

"What makes you think I really like him?" I ask.

"Because you never show interest in *any-one*. Trust me, I've watched over the years as poor souls tried their damndest to get your attention, and you never gave any of them a second glance. You've been in California a few weeks, and you've fallen into bed with someone; that means he must be something special. Did Pax introduce you to him? Is it one of his friends? Because if he let one of his friends treat you that way, I'm going to kick his ass."

My throat tightens. "It's not Pax's fault."

Theo scoffs, and then I hear the sound of a buzzer on his end of the phone.

"Shit, my date's here. Are you okay? Because if you still need to talk or you just want to sit on the phone, not saying anything to each other while we both watch Netflix, I can cancel this date, and I'm all yours."

"I'm okay. Go on your date, have a good time."

"Are you sure?" he asks again.

"I'm sure. I'll talk to you later."

Pax

The loud chatter and even louder music in the bar swirl together to create a kind of white noise. I watch a bead of condensation trickle down the side of the glass to pool on the grainy wood of the table.

A sharp elbow catches me in the ribs, and I look up to find three sets of curious, concerned eyes on me.

"I'm sorry, what?" I ask, not having the slightest clue what I missed while I was spacing out.

"We were asking what's been keeping you so busy the past few weeks," Seph says, rolling the little black straw in her drink back and forth between her teeth, her bright blue eyes fixed on me inquisitively.

"I guessed it was probably work since we all know there's no way it's a guy keeping your attention this thoroughly," Hudson jokes, elbowing me again playfully.

"And I said maybe you're just sick of us," Bishop adds with a self-deprecating laugh.

I met the three of them the first week I moved to California. I was scoping out the action at Twisted Cherry, and Bishop caught my eye, and I'd sauntered over to lay on the charm. It didn't take more than thirty seconds for Hudson to shut me down and Seph to laugh hysterically at my pick-up attempt. Somehow that turned into some of the best friendships I've ever had, even if they do like to bust my balls.

"I'm not sick of you guys," I assure them. "I was doing a favor for my brother. His best friend moved to town a few weeks ago to go to CalTech, and he asked me to help him get the lay of the land, show him where the good bars are, that kind of thing."

"CalTech, wow," Seph says. "He must be a super nerd. Is he cute?" Her eyes light up with interest. She's a self-proclaimed sapiosexual, or as she puts it, she doesn't care what's between someone's legs, only what's between their ears.

"Keep it in your pants Persephone James," I scold, and she sticks out her bottom lip in a pout.

"Fine, keep the hot genius all to yourself," she huffs.

"You afraid we were going to scare him or what?" Hudson asks, eyebrows raised.

"Or afraid you'd hit on the poor kid," Bishop mutters, his tone saltier than the rim of his margarita glass. Six years of friendship with them and I've never been able to figure out exactly what the deal is between Hudson and Bishop, but I'd put money on them having slept together at some point.

Hudson ignores the jab, and Bishop takes a big gulp of his drink, Seph watching the entire scene with humor dancing in her eyes.

"I don't blame you from trying to shield the kid from Hudson's advances, but you should totally invite him out with us. Bishop and I can fend Hudson off if he becomes feral."

I snort and take a sip of my own drink. "I wasn't worried about Horndog Hudson," I assure them. "He's really shy so I didn't want to overwhelm him."

"Oh, well, if you decide to bring him around, I promise we'll all be on our best behavior. Hey, we could do like a low-key dinner party like proper adults," Seph suggests, perking up with excitement at her own idea. "Oh, please, let me throw a dinner party. It'll be so classy."

"I'm not sure any of us would be very good at classy," I lament.

"No, shut up, I'm doing it," she declares, pulling out her phone, presumably to check her calendar app. "Next Saturday, everyone put it on your schedule. I'll get fancy wine, and I'll cook tiny little game hens or something equally as posh. It'll be great."

"Tiny food, sounds fantastic," Hudson says sarcastically.

"I think it sounds really nice," Bishop offers.

"Thank you. I'm glad *someone* around here appreciates my effort," Seph says, giving Bishop a side hug and shooting a venomous glare at Hudson before turning her attention back to me. "So, will you invite him? He can be our guest of honor."

"I don't know." I gulp down the rest of my drink and set the glass back down on the table harder than intended. I haven't spoken to Elijah all week. Every time I picked up my phone to text him, all I could think about was how his skin felt against mine and the sound of his breathy moans. Goosebumps prickle up my arm at the thought, my cock shifting in my jeans. The problem is, I *want* to text him. I want to find a way to reset things back to the way they were before last weekend.

"Why not?" Hudson asks.

"He's pretty busy with school and everything; I'm not sure he'll have time."

"It doesn't hurt to ask," Seph points out. "Besides, he has to eat, it might as well be fancy, tiny birds."

I bite back a laugh at Seph's single mindedness. "I'll ask him, but I'm not making any guarantees. But even if he can't make it, there's no reason we can't have our own fancy-ass dinner party."

"Here, here." She raises her glass, and Bishop obliges in toasting her.

When the conversation finally turns away from Elijah and to complaints about work and life, I let my mind wander again. I start to feel like a complete dick for ghosting Elijah all week. I get why Theo has been protective of him all these years—he just brings out something in you that makes you want to shield him from the big bad world. The thought of him at home alone tonight, wondering why I haven't called or texted, twists in my gut like a knife, and I reach for my phone.

Pax: Hey Einstein, sorry I haven't texted all week, I was crazy busy wooing a client down in Florida

I have no doubt he'll see right through the excuse. I'm always busy with clients, but it hasn't stopped me from texting before this week. I'm hoping he'll take it as an olive branch anyway and let me off the hook. My heart pounds as I wait for his reply. I wouldn't blame him if he decides to ignore me. Hell, it's probably what I deserve after being the asshole who pulled a fuck and run on him last weekend or at least the frotting equivalent of it.

When the little dots appear, I let out the breath I was holding, my hand clenching tight around my phone as I wait to see what he'll say.

Einstein: No big deal, I was busy all week too, so it worked out

My chest clenches. I swear I can practically see the defiant set of his jaw through the phone, an expression stubbornly in place to convince me he didn't even notice I hadn't texted.

Pax: What are you up to tonight?
Einstein: Studying. You? Flirting with cute guys at the bar, I'm guessing?

I should lie and tell him that's exactly what I'm doing. Hell, it's what I *should* be doing. The sooner he sees who I really am, the easier things will be.

Pax: Nah, just hanging with some friends. I'm kind of bored though, thinking about heading home…

I'm not fishing for an invite to him place. Of course I'm not.

Einstein: Oh

I wait to see if he'll say anything else, and when he doesn't, I consider leaving it alone. If it was Hudson or Bishop or Seph, I'd leave it at that. Although, I've gone half a decade without humping any of them into oblivion, so clearly, it's not an apples to oranges type of comparison.

Pax: You eat yet?

It's after ten, so I'm sure he has.

Einstein: Just popcorn. I kind of lost track of the time.

A smile spreads slowly across my lips.
"Texting your nerdy boy? Is there something here you're not telling us because I've *never* seen you that focused on your phone," Seph asks.
"No," I lie. "I'm feeling a bit wiped. This week took it out of me. I think I'm going to call it an early night."
"Now who's going to be my wingman?"

Hudson complains.

"I'm sure you'll find a way to trick unsuspecting men into your bed without my help," I assure him, patting his shoulder.

"I'll catch you guys next week for our fancy dinner party."

"Hell yeah, you will," Seph cheers.

On my way out of the bar, I send one more text.

Pax: Be there in twenty with a pizza
Einstein: Ok

CHAPTER 10

Elijah

I glance down at myself. I'm dressed in a plain white t-shirt and a pair of gray sweatpants. It was a perfectly acceptable outfit for sitting at home by myself on a Friday night, but now that I'll be sitting at home with Pax, do I need to change? It would be weird if he showed up to sit around and eat pizza and I'm dressed like I'm ready to go out. I don't want it to look like I'm trying to impress him.

I bite my lip and fiddle with the hem of my shirt. I'd call Theo back and ask his opinion, but I don't want to interrupt his date.

When the buzzer sounds to announce Pax's arrival, I'm still in my sweatpants, and I decide that's just how it's going to have to stay. I wipe my sweaty hands on my pants and hit the button to let him into the building, and then I hurry over to my table to clear off all my textbooks and papers.

The front door creaks open a minute later, and Pax pops his head in, a big, cocky smile on his lips. He's dressed like he always is, in a dress shirt, sleeves rolled up. His hair is styled neatly, and, when he gets close, I can smell the distinct scent of the bar on him.

Was he really out with friends or was he looking for a hookup? Not that I have any business wondering about it. And if he *was* at the bar looking for someone to take home, what's he doing here?

Pax's eyes latch onto mine, and my stomach squirms. There's heat in his gaze I don't understand. He made it clear he wasn't interested in me like *that*. I think I need a new principle of physics to figure this one out. If Heisenberg's Uncertainty principle is that you can know the velocity or location of an object at any given time, but not both. I think the Paxton Uncertainty principle has to be that you can understand what he says or how he acts, but both can't be comprehensible at the same time.

"Um...thanks for the pizza," I say, reaching for the box in his hand. The heat leaches out of his expression, and it's replaced with what appears to be guilt that I can't begin to understand. I wonder for a second if he thinks he took advantage of me last weekend. I want to set him straight, in case that's the reason behind how distant he's been all week, but I can't think of how to bring it up in a way that isn't devastatingly embarrassing, so I don't say anything.

"Why don't we put on some old horror sci-fi and eat in front of the TV like heathens?" Pax suggests when I set the pizza down at the table.

"Oh, yeah, that sounds nice," I agree, smoothing my shirt with my hands simply to have something to do with them. The only consolation is that he seems just as uncomfortable as I am. I wonder how people do this, hook up with people casually and then see them again later without being completely awkward messes. In college, Theo messed around with guys who lived on our dorm floor all the time, and he never seemed to get weird about it.

We get comfortable on the couch, a few feet between us, and pick out a movie. I shift around, trying not to think about the last time we were on this couch together and how his lips felt on mine. My heart beats faster at the thought, and I pray that Pax won't notice the semi I'm sporting.

"My friends were asking about where I've been lately," he says as we each grab a slice of pizza.

"Oh?" I'm not sure if I'm supposed to apologize for monopolizing his weekends lately or if he's simply stating a fact.

"I told them a little about you," he goes on.

"Oh?" I say again, heat rising in my cheeks. What could he have possibly told them about me? Surely not what happened between us last weekend, right? Although it's common practice to tell friends about...those kinds of things. At least I think it is. Theo always told me about his hookups in graphic detail, even when I tried to get him to stop.

Oh my god, what if he told them I'm horrible in bed? The thought makes me feel sick to my stomach. I mean, I'm sure I wasn't all that great, but it was my *first* time. My first rocket didn't fly either. Some things take a little time to get exactly right.

"Yeah, I told them you're Theo's best friend, and you just moved out here to go to CalTech."

"Oh," this one is said with a breath of relief, my shoulders sagging.

"They want to meet you. Persephone, we call her Seph, she got this idea in her head to throw some kind of dinner party next weekend."

"They want to meet me? Why?"

Pax shrugs, taking a big bite of his pizza. "They're my friends, you're my friend, it makes sense."

"It does?" I swallow hard, nerves making my stomach flutter too hard to risk taking a bite of pizza. "I never met any of Theo's other friends. I mean, at first he tried introducing me, but most of the time they'd end up making fun of me and then Theo would yell at them and never see them again. After a while, he stopped introducing me to them. I think he got sick of having to defend me," I confess, curling in on myself a little at the memory.

He reaches over with his free hand and

tilts my chin up, forcing me to meet his eyes.

"First of all, I am absolutely positive Theo wasn't sick of defending you. If anything, he probably started to feel bad that you kept ending up in situations that hurt your feelings," he says. "And second, I guarantee my friends won't make fun of you. If anything, I'm more worried that two out of three of them will try to get in your pants."

My eyebrows pull together, and I tilt my head. "Why would they want to do that? I'm nothing special to look at. I'm awkward, I'm... there's no reason for anyone to want me that way."

Pain lances through Pax's eyes, and for a few stuttered heartbeats, I'm sure he's about to kiss me.

"Oh, Einstein, you really have no idea."

Pax

I've never wanted to kiss someone so badly in my life. Truth be told, most of the time I could take or leave kissing. But I swear to fuck there's nothing I want more right now than to kiss that insecure little pout off Elijah's lips. The feeling hits me so hard in the chest I can hardly breathe for a few seconds.

But I can't do it. I *won't* do it to him...or to Theo—if my assumption is correct that he has a thing for Elijah. Even without my brother being a possible issue, Elijah deserves better than what

I can give him. I've tried the whole relationship thing, and I've been an utter failure at it.

"So, you'll come next Saturday?" I ask, hoping to deflect from the weight of the moment hanging between us.

"I guess," he agrees. "Why not."

"That's the spirit," I tease, taking another bite of my pizza and settling back on the couch. He picks up his own slice again and nibbles at the end cautiously before eventually relaxing into the couch and taking a larger bite.

I let my gaze roam over him for a few seconds, taking in his casual attire. It looks just as good on him as the blazers. I try for a few seconds to pull up the image of a single man at the bar tonight who might've caught my interest, and I come up completely blank. I don't think I even looked around; I just stared at my phone and thought about Elijah.

An uncomfortable ache starts in my chest, and I ease it with another slice of pizza as I turn my attention to whatever it is he put on the TV. But I can't seem to focus on anything except the man less than two feet away on the other end of the couch.

What is wrong with me? It was a meaningless hookup, nothing more. I've never had trouble keeping this shit in perspective or separating physical from feelings.

"Can I ask you a question?" he asks. I pull my gaze away from the television—not that I was actually watching it—and look over at him again. His cheeks are already pink, his eyes wide and innocent like he's fucking *trying* to be as irresistible as possible.

"Sure, Nerdlet, shoot."

"I was wondering if you'd still help me learn how to flirt? Because I was kind of thinking...I um...I kind of want to maybe...you know, find someone."

My heart constricts, and my stomach churns, threatening to send the pizza I just swallowed back up.

"Oh?" I guess I'm stealing Elijah's lines now, but I can't think of a damn thing to say to that. I told him we're friends, and I meant it. I wingman for Hudson all the time without batting an eye, and it shouldn't be any different with helping Elijah hookup or date or whatever the hell he wants to do.

"Yeah, I've never thought that much about dating. It's always seemed like more of a hassle than it's worth. Plus, all the stress of trying to figure out if someone likes me and everything. But maybe if you help me, I could get it right?" He bites his bottom lip and looks at me with hopeful eyes.

"Sure," I say before I can think about it. You'd have to be a heartless monster to say no to a face like that, but goddamn do I *not* want to do this. Elijah can date, he *should* date, especially someone other than me. But I don't want to have to see it, and I definitely don't want to *help*.

A slow smile spreads over his lips.

"Thanks, Pax."

"Sure, Nerdlet."

CHAPTER 11

Elijah

Elijah: What are you wearing?
Pax: Nothing but a smile ;)
Elijah: What?
Elijah: Oh my god, I meant seriously, what are you wearing to the dinner party?
Pax: That's unfortunate, I was so excited you'd gotten the hang of flirting for a second
Elijah: No, and don't hold your breath for that to happen any time soon.
Pax: What you normally wear is fine. You look hot in your stylish blazers

Heat creeps into my cheeks, and I'm glad he can't see how hard I'm blushing. I'm sure he didn't mean anything by it—he's a flirt. But it still feels nice to hear that Pax might think I look nice.

Elijah: Ok. I'll be ready in twenty minutes then
Pax: Well that's good because I'm standing outside

Elijah: What? Why didn't you say that before?

Pax: Because I thought you were flirting with me, and I didn't want to interrupt

Elijah: And people think I'm the weird one. I'll buzz you up, give me one second

I hit the buzzer and unlock my door so he can come right in when he gets up here, then I turn my attention back to my clothes, trying to decide what to wear to this, quote, *fancy-ass dinner party*.

"I like the white blazer with the thin gray stripes, with that white t-shirt. I think it's what you were wearing the first night we met at Twisted Cherry," Pax says from behind me, making me jump.

"Jeez, I didn't even hear you come in. You nearly gave me a heart attack." I put a hand over my chest. It takes me a few seconds to fully catch up to what he just said. Pax remembers what I was wearing one night over a month ago?

I reach for the items he suggested, and he hops onto my bed and makes himself comfortable.

"Do you mind? I need to get dressed."

"I don't mind," he purrs suggestively, smirking as he lets his eyes roam over my fully clothed body in a way that makes me feel completely naked. I drop my gaze as my heart starts to beat faster again—this time it has nothing to do with fear. "It's not like I haven't seen it all anyway, Einstein."

I sputter and blush, doing my best to ignore the heat that pools between my legs, my cock hardening at the reminder.

"That was different. I was too distracted to feel self-conscious about how pale and skinny I am," I argue. I still don't know the exact reason Pax wasn't interested in a repeat, but I'm sure my unsexy body was somewhere on the list.

"Elijah," he says my name in a deep rumble, his tone holding a seriousness that isn't typical for him. I look up, and his eyes are on me again, or maybe still, but instead of pure heat, there's a depth in his gaze I didn't expect. "You're hot as fuck. The way you look has *nothing* to do with why I don't think it's a good idea to fool around again," he explains as if he read my thoughts.

"I know," I lie. "It's fine. We don't need to talk about it."

I strip my shirt over my head and toss it toward the laundry hamper, resisting the urge to wrap my arms around myself to hide. I don't look at Pax, but I can feel his eyes on me every second it takes me to dress.

I don't bother to do much with my hair aside from run a quick comb through it. Honestly, it's hopeless to do much more than that anyway.

"All right, let's get this over with," I say,

squaring my shoulders.

Pax snorts a laugh. "Relax, Nerdlet, it's dinner with my friends, not a firing squad."

"Feels like the same thing," I murmur, running my hands over my blazer to smooth out any imaginary wrinkles.

He gets up off my bed, moving to stand directly in front of me. He puts a hand under my chin and tilts my face up so I'm forced to look at him, my heart in my throat. The heat is back in his eyes, and for a crazy moment I wonder if he's going to kiss me again. If I was the praying type, I might even spare a prayer for it to happen, just *one* more time. I'm already starting to forget the taste of his lips, and if that's not a tragedy, I'm not sure what is.

"I promise tonight will be fun. And if you're miserable, you say the word, and we're out of there."

"Really?" I ask, a smile tugging at the corner of my lips. "What word should I say? Do we need a special code word?"

"Sure, we can have a code word," he agrees. "How about sugar tits?"

I snort and roll my eyes. "I'm *not* saying that."

"That's exactly why it's the perfect code word; you're not going to accidentally say it in conversation," he reasons.

"No."

"Fine. Ball sac?" he suggests.

"You are officially *not* in charge of the code word," I say. "Our code word is quantum optics."

"Are you sure you won't accidentally use that in casual conversation?" he deadpans.

"Hmm, good point. It *could* come up. Okay, here it is, final code phrase: Paxton is a genius. There's *no* way *that* could be said in casual conversation."

"Ha. Ha," he says blandly. "Fine, code phrase decided upon. Can we go now?"

"Yes, let's go."

Pax

Every time Elijah fiddles with his blazer on our drive over to Seph's place, I have a harder time remembering *why* I'm not supposed to want to pull over and kiss the hell out of him.

"Relax, Einstein," I say, reaching over to put my hand over his to stop his fidgeting.

He stills under my touch, his skin warm and smooth under my fingers, reminding me of how the rest of him felt. Goddamn, it should *not* be this difficult to stop thinking about one fucking hookup. It's done and over with, and it's not going to happen again.

Pulling into the driveway of the little ranch house Seph has been renting for the past few years, I park the car and unbuckle before turning to look at Elijah. His face is pale in the dim light of the evening, his fingers shaking as he reaches to unbuckle his own seatbelt. I search my mind for a way to reassure him again, but I've said everything there is to say. He needs to see that they're good people, then he'll relax. But the fact that he's clearly had enough bad experiences to make him *this* nervous makes me want to rip somebody's head off.

"Come on, I'm starving," I encourage, climbing out of the car.

It takes a few seconds before he follows, but eventually he gets out, and we meet at the front of the car. Without thinking, I drop my hand to his lower back, and for a fraction of a second, he leans into my touch before starting forward toward the house.

As soon as we set foot on the front porch, the door flies open, and Seph greets us dressed like a fifties housewife in a black and white polka dot dress, a red, frilly apron around her waist, her hair styled and full makeup on. It's a major departure from the usually laid back look she tends to prefer.

"What the hell happened to you?" I ask, and her smile turns to a scowl, and she punches me in the shoulder. "Ow, damn, I just meant you look different than you usually do."

"I think you look really nice," Elijah offers in a quiet, sheepish voice.

"Thank you," Seph says, beaming at him before giving me another glare. "Your friend can stay, you can leave."

"Aw, don't be salty, Sephy. I didn't say you

didn't look nice." I give her my best boyish grin, snagging her around the waist and forcing a hug on her.

"You're an ass," she declares, giving into the hug after a moment of token struggle. "Come on in. I've been slaving away for hours."

I release her and give Elijah a reassuring look before following her inside.

I have to admit, it smells amazing as we make our way down the hallway to the eat-in kitchen. Bishop and Hudson are already there, leaning against the counter, each with a glass of wine in hand. It seems like they're in a whispered argument that abruptly ends when they realize they're no longer alone.

"Seph is forcing us to drink wine," Hudson says in way of greeting.

"I'm not *forcing* you to do anything," she argues.

"You wouldn't let us have beer."

"Because beer isn't fancy," she points out as if that settles it. "You can have water if you'd prefer."

Hudson makes a face, and Bishop takes a sip from his own glass. "It's good wine, and it adds to the ambiance," he says.

Hudson snorts a laugh. "You're only agreeing with her because you're pissed off at me."

"Self-absorbed much? I'm capable of thoughts and feelings that have nothing whatsoever to do with you," Bishop grumbles.

"Yeah, you've made that *perfectly* clear."

My eyes ping pong between the two of them as they snipe at each other, and I wonder, not for the first time, if there's more than friendship there.

"*Okay*," I say to draw everyone's attention. "Let's not scare Elijah away in the first five minutes, all right?"

"Sorry, Elijah," Bishop apologizes, crossing the kitchen with a friendly smile, his hand extended. "You'll have to forgive Hudson, he's not housebroken yet."

Elijah gives a quiet laugh and takes Bishop's hand. Hudson and Seph officially introduce themselves next, and I can see Elijah start to visibly relax.

Seph gets us each a glass of wine and tells us dinner should be ready in about ten minutes.

"I can't believe you left early last weekend, man," Hudson says. "A group of undergrads stumbled in about an hour after you took off, and I had to take three of them home all by myself since you weren't there to help out." He smirks, and out of the corner of my eye, I catch Bishop wince.

"I'm sure that was quite a hardship for you," I tease. "Those poor guys though, stuck with you instead of the thousands of better options they could've gone home with instead."

"Fuck you," he chuckles. "Where'd you need to take off to so early anyway? You don't actually expect us to believe you went home that early just to go to bed by yourself, do you?"

I cast a quick glance in Elijah's direction and see him intensely focused on his wine glass.

I clear my throat, casting around for an excuse. I can't tell them I ditched out early to go eat pizza and watch old sci-fi movies with Elijah. It will sound like there's something going on between us that there's not. They'll never let it go if they get that impression.

"Grindr hookup," I lie.

"Oh yeah? Tell us about him," Hudson prompts. "Was he as slutty as the last one you told me about? Getting on his knees and begging for your cock before you even had the door closed?"

I want to look over at Elijah so badly to gauge his reaction, but I force myself to hold Hudson's curious gaze, a fake lazy smile spreading over my lips.

"Something like that."

"Come on, you've gotta give me more than that," he pushes.

"Leave it alone, Hudson. Maybe he doesn't want to talk about it," Bishop scolds.

"But he *always* wants to talk about the guys he fucks," Hudson argues, and I finally give in to the urge and glance over at Elijah. His cheeks are pink, and his eyes are still trained on his wine glass, his shoulders slightly hunched as he leans against the counter, not saying a word.

"I don't tell you about all my hookups," I argue weakly. Prior to two weeks ago that would've been a lie, but I didn't tell them about Elijah, and I have no plans to. And not just because I don't need the grief. In a weird way, it feels too private to tell anyone about. Wow, maybe I'm maturing or some shit like that.

"Dinner's ready, you heathens," Seph declares.

I have to admit, the tiny ass birds she cooked are delicious, as is the rest of the meal. Everyone does their best to include Elijah in the conversation, and I'm extremely grateful for that. There's the normal amount of ribbing and gutter talk, which Seph scowls about, declaring it not suitable for her dinner party. But by the end of the night we're all full and relaxed, and I think we'd all have to say Seph was right about a dinner party being fun.

Elijah is quiet when we get back into the car a few hours later.

"That wasn't so bad, right?" I ask.

"It was all right," he says vaguely.

"They were all nice, and the food was good," I prompt, hoping he'll tell me he had a great time and can't wait to hang out with my friends again. I'm not sure why it's so important to me, but I want to know he liked them.

"They were great, it's just..." he cuts himself off, shaking his head and slouching in his seat.

"It's just what?"

"I don't get you. That first night at the bar with the *Star Wars* argument, you were so passionate and smart. You've been the same when you come to hang out at my place or text me. But then tonight you're this dude-bro asshole who only thinks with his dick. It's like you're some kind of horny Dr. Jekyll and Mr. Hyde."

His words hit their mark in the center of my chest, making me wince.

"Haven't you ever wanted to be someone else?" I ask.

I expect the answer to come quickly. He's a socially awkward genius, of course he must've daydreamed about being like everyone else. When he doesn't respond right away, I look over and catch him chewing his bottom lip, seemingly deep in thought. His gaze flicks to mine and ensnares me.

"No," he answers. "As much as it has always sucked to be laughed at and misunderstood, I wouldn't trade who I am just to fit in."

My gut twists and a pained, self-loathing smile twists on my lips. "I guess you're a better man than me."

Neither of us say anything the entire drive back to Elijah's apartment, his words echoing in my head. Maybe tonight was a bad idea. Around Elijah these past few weeks I almost forgot who I really am. The guy I am around Hudson, Bishop, and Seph, that's the real Paxton—a horny asshole with no business wanting someone as innocent as Elijah.

I pull up in front of his building, and he unbuckles but pauses before getting out.

"I'm sorry, I didn't mean to come off as judgmental or anything. I was caught off guard because you were so different tonight."

"I'm sorry too. I hope you still had a good time."

A shy smile tilts the corner of his lips. "I did, actually. They were nice and kind of funny."

"Yeah, they are," I agree. "I'll see you next weekend?" I ask.

He scrunches his eyebrows and tilts his head. "What's next weekend?"

"I don't know, Nerdlet," I answer with a smirk. "I guess we'll have to think of something."

"Okay," he agrees, and I watch as he finally gets out of the car. I watch him the entire way up the steps to his building, and it's not until I see the light in his unit come on that I pull away.

CHAPTER 12

Elijah

"Hey, what are you doing this weekend?" Alex asks as soon as class ends, falling into step beside me as we make our way to our next class.

"Um…" I push my glasses up my nose. Pax said he wanted to hang out again this weekend, but it felt like things were a little strange between us when he dropped me off. Not that I'm an expert on social situations or anything, but it seemed like there was a weird tension between us. We've been texting a little this week, but it's felt stilted, not like before. On the other hand, at least there *was* communication, unlike the week before. Maybe everyone is right when they say sex ruins friendships. I didn't even get full on sex before the friendship was ruined. I feel kind of ripped off.

"Earth to Elijah." Alex waves his hand in front of my face and chuckles. "This weekend? Friday to be specific? What are your plans?"

"I'm not sure," I finally answer. "Hanging out with a friend, I think, but I don't know what we're doing." Will he want to order takeout and watch Netflix or drag me out to another bar in an attempt to hone my flirting skills? If it's the latter, it's my own fault. I'm the one who told him I still wanted help learning to flirt. I don't even know why I said it. I don't want to flirt with anyone else, and I *definitely* don't want to do with anyone else what I did with Pax.

"Jeez, you really are off in La-La Land today, aren't you?" Alex laughs.

"I'm sorry, what?"

"I asked if you wanted to come to a party I'm throwing. You can bring your friend," he offers. "It's going to be pretty low key, but it should be fun."

"A party?"

"Yeah, you know drinks, food, people mingling." He smirks at me.

"Oh, I don't know." I push my glasses up again, heat rising in my face, steaming them up.

"Tell you what, I'll text you my address, and if you find yourself trying to find something to do on Friday night, you can swing by."

"Sure," I agree, already knowing hell will freeze over before I go to a party.

Pax

As soon as I drop my suitcase and computer bag on my bed, I reach into my pocket and grab my phone with a singular focus.

Pax: Just got home, jumping in the shower

123

and then swinging by
Einstein: Ok, should I get ready to go out somewhere or....?

I consider the question while I strip out of my clothes, tossing them into my hamper. Is he asking to go out so I can help him with his flirting skills more like we talked about a couple of weeks ago?

Pax: Let's stay in
Einstein: Ok, see you soon

When I get to Elijah's he buzzes me up and is waiting with the door open when I make it up to his floor. He's gripping the door tightly, his knuckles white, a tense smile on his lips. Fucking hell, what's it going to take to get back on even footing?

For a crazy second I consider kissing the painful expression off of him.

"Come on in," he says. "I ordered Chinese food."

"Great."

I follow him into the apartment and plop down on the couch while he heads to the kitchen area.

Elijah's phone buzzes on the coffee table, and because I'm shameless and curious, I lean forward to see what the notification says. Text from Alex. Who the hell is Alex? Some guy he's been hanging out with during the week while I'm away? A girl in his classes? Why the hell do I even care? But regardless of the lack of logic in my reaction, my jaw ticks.

"You've got a text," I call as he stands in the kitchen pulling our food out of the paper bags it came in.

"I do?" He sounds surprised, which eases some of my jealousy, replacing it with that warm affection I've come to associate with how adorably clueless my little Nerdlet is. Well, not *mine*...

"Yeah, it says it's from Alex," I say, and he groans. "Who's Alex?"

"Just a guy," he answers, spiking my blood pressure again.

"A guy?"

"Yeah, from school. He reminds me of Theo, all petite and way more confident that I could ever dream of being. I guess we're kind of friends?"

I let out a relieved laugh. "That's cool. Maybe he's texting you to hang out? It *is* the weekend after all. Even super geniuses need weekends off."

"Um...yeah." He carries over the boxes of Chinese food and a couple of forks, his face carefully blank.

"What?" I ask suspiciously.

"What?" he repeats, his expression full of innocence, that for once looks fake.

"You're being cagey, you already know what the text says?"

"It's probably a reminder that he's having a party tonight that he wanted me to come to," Elijah admits, his gaze intensely focused on his container of chicken fried rice.

"A party? Why didn't you say so? I can go find a way to entertain myself while you go make some new friends." It's what Theo wanted for him, right? And my brother's known Elijah long enough to know what's best for him.

He shakes his head rapidly, shoving a forkful of food into his mouth. "He said you could come too, but I don't think it's a good idea."

"I'm invited too?" A slow smile spreads across my lips. "Even better. We're doing this. Food first and then we're going to the party. I'm dying to see if college parties have changed since my day."

"It's not like a *college* party. It's probably going to be a bunch of grad students from CalTech, not exactly the wildest crowd," he argues, clearly trying to deter my excitement.

"Sounds like a blast," I lie. Being with Elijah is *always* a blast, and I'm sure the party won't be half bad.

"This is *not* how you want to spend a Friday night," he argues, fixing me with a leveling stare.

"Oh, but it is," I contradict with a smirk. "Food first, then we party."

He groans again. "No."

"Yes," I insist, chuckling when he makes another pained sound.

"You're worse than Theo," he complains, picking up an eggroll and biting into it aggressively.

"Oh yeah? Are you going to call my brother and tattle that I'm not being nice to you?"

"Yes, and he'll probably fly out here and kick your ass," he threatens with a grin.

"I'm sure," I say deadpan. I wonder for the dozenth time about Theo's feelings toward Elijah. Even if he only sees him as a friend, he trusted me to watch out for him, not get him naked and then do a one-eighty as soon as the cum cools. Guilt swamps me, making the food in my stomach feel like a brick.

"I didn't tell him, if that's what you're worried about. I mean, I told him there was *someone*, but I didn't tell him it was you."

"Oh yeah, and how'd he take that?" I ask, keeping my voice even.

Elijah shrugs. "He was worried about me, but otherwise fine. He gets overprotective sometimes, but I know he only has my best interest at heart."

"Yeah," I agree, setting aside my mostly uneaten food. "I'm not all that hungry, why don't we put this stuff in the fridge for later and get over to that party."

CHAPTER 13

Elijah

My heart is beating so hard I'm wondering if it's possible for it to bruise a rib. As we climb the steps to Alex's apartment, Pax puts a hand on my lower back, and even though I'm sure it's meant to soothe my nerves, it only serves to make me claustrophobic. My knees start to tremble with each step that takes us closer to the second floor.

Memories of mocking laughter, sneering faces, humiliation so complete it still makes me sick to my stomach to this day, all flood my mind and make bile rise in my throat.

"I changed my mind; let's skip this party." I try to turn around and head back down the stairs, but Pax stands in my way.

"We're already here, Einstein. Let's just pop in for a bit and see how it goes."

My lungs feel too tight as I attempt to drag in a complete breath. All I can do is shake my head as I reach for the railing, wrapping my fingers around it so tightly they start to go numb.

"Hey, hey." Pax reaches for me again but draws up short like he's not sure how or where to touch me. "It's okay, just breathe."

I shake my head again and squeeze my eyes closed.

"I don't want to do this."

"All right, why don't you sit down for a second and catch your breath first," he suggests, using his hands to steady me as I slide down to plop myself down on the step. I lean forward, putting my head between my knees and forcing myself to draw in deeper breaths, holding them for five seconds each before releasing them. Pax sits down next to me, his hand going to my back, rubbing circles right between my shoulder blades. I lean into his touch, enjoying the warmth of it, even if I know I shouldn't.

Once my breathing returns to normal, I lift my head and look over at him, his expression patient but filled with concern.

"In high school, there was this party," I say, figuring the least I can do is explain my freak out. "It was the same weekend as your college graduation, so Theo was out of town with your parents. Normally, I wouldn't have gone without him, but for some reason I thought it might be fun." My throat tightens, and I swallow hard, leaning into Pax's touch.

"What happened?"

"As soon as I got there, the guy who was throwing the party, Patrick, got me a drink and took me over to talk to his friends. I thought it was going really well. I was proud of myself for putting myself out there for a change. Then Patrick started flirting with me."

Pax's expression darkens but he doesn't say anything, just waits for me to go on.

"I didn't particularly like him, but he was cute enough, and since I'd never even kissed someone before, I figured it couldn't hurt anything to go with it and see what might happen. He kept giving me drinks, touching me...it was nice." I swallow around the lump in my throat again, licking my lips to try and moisten my dry mouth. I tug at the sleeve of my blazer, dropping my gaze because I don't think I can look at Pax while I tell him the next part.

"Did he...force you to do something?" he asks, his voice low and dangerous like the rumble of thunder from a distant storm.

"No, nothing like that," I assure him. "He took me out on the back porch, and I thought he was going to kiss me. When I leaned in, someone came up behind me and yanked my pants and underwear down. Patrick laughed and started taking pictures, making fun of the fact that I'd tried to kiss him and that I was hard, calling me...well, I'm sure you can guess."

"That little prick," he growls.

"Yeah," I agree with a sigh. "He sent the pictures to everyone and people pretty much made fun of me for it for the rest of high school. I also got grounded for the summer for coming home drunk. That was the last time I went to a party."

"Those guys were fucking assholes—it doesn't mean everyone is," he says. "Maybe this is one of those times when you need to try getting back up on the horse? I'm here, and there's no way I'll let anything like that happen to you. We can go in there, and you can see that parties don't have to end with years of torment."

I bite my bottom lip and finally look over at him again, torn between wanting to run home to the safety of my apartment and wanting to do something as painfully normal as going to a college party. It's not like this is a frat party, and Alex doesn't seem to be anything like Patrick or his friends. And I *do* trust Pax to protect me.

"Can I use the code phrase if it sucks, and I want to leave?"

Pax chuckles, his hand drifting from my hand to the back of my neck, giving it a small squeeze that manages to heat my entire body all at once.

"Yes, you can use the code phrase," he agrees.

"All right," I agree, taking a deep breath and grabbing the railing again to pull myself up. "Let's get this over with."

We climb the last few steps and head down the hallway until we find the right apartment number. The sound of voices and soft music filter out into the hallway, and my stomach flips and twists itself with nerves.

"You've got this; it's going to be fine," Pax encourages.

I take another deep breath, raise my fist, and knock. It only takes a few seconds before the door swings open, and Alex greets us with a huge smile.

"Oh my god, I'm so glad you made it," he says, throwing his arms around me in what's probably the most aggressive hug I've ever experienced. I shoot Pax a panicked look.

"Pax is a genius," I gasp as Alex squeezes me, and Pax hides a laugh behind a fake cough.

"What?" Alex asks, finally releasing me and cutting his gaze over to Pax. "Oh my, who do we have here?" He looks Pax up and down like he's a dessert I brought with me.

I bristle and step in front of Pax in an attempt to shield him from Alex's view.

"This is my friend, Paxton. I hope it's okay I brought him with me."

"It's *more* than okay," he purrs, and Pax does the coughing laugh thing again behind me. Something tells me this is going to be a long night.

Alex leads us into the kitchen, introducing us to several people along the way. It's nothing like Patrick's party. Yes, everyone seems to be drinking, but it's not rowdy like I expected. I recognize a number of people I've seen in passing on campus or in class, and the rest look like they fit in with the same crowd. This isn't a frat party; it's a nerd party, and I can get on board with that.

I take a wine cooler when offered, but Pax sticks to water, which relaxes me a bit. I know he'll be clear headed if anything happens.

"Sorry, this party doesn't seem much like your scene," I say to Pax once Alex leaves us to go answer the door again.

He shrugs. "You're here, that makes it my scene."

Heat rises in my cheeks, and I take a sip of my drink to hide my smile. I know he doesn't mean it the way it sounds, but it's difficult to tell my heart that as it tries to leap out of my chest.

Alex returns a few minutes later, and he's all smiles and fluttering eyelashes for Pax again. The worst part is, Pax doesn't seem to mind it at all. He flirts right back, seeming to forget I'm standing there at all as he jokes and laughs with Alex.

The knots in my stomach are back. I can understand Pax not wanting me, but what is it that makes Alex different? I study their inter-action, trying to figure out what exactly it is, but eventually I can't take it anymore. I set my empty wine cooler down and slip out of the kit-chen without anyone even noticing.

Pax

I manage to break away from the flirty

twink Elijah introduced as Alex, and I realize Elijah is gone. I check the living room and the kitchen, where everyone seems to be congregated for the most part. It's definitely a nerd party, that's for sure—I swear to god a game of D&D seems to have broken out at the kitchen table, and that's the kind of shit you just can't make up. I have to admit, there's a nice vibe in the place though. Sure, people are drinking, but it's not the kind of raucous, alcohol fueled sex-fest that all the college parties I went to were.

When I find the bathroom unoccupied, the only place left to check for Elijah is in the bedrooms. I find the first two totally empty—again, weird for a party if you ask me—but strike gold on try number three.

The room is dark, an outside streetlamp the only light illuminating the dark shape on the bed. He sits up as I step into the room but doesn't say anything.

"Everything okay?" I check.

"Fine," he answers.

"Are you sure? Because you're kind of sitting alone in a dark room instead of enjoying the party," I point out. He scoots to the end of the bed and stands up. I can't make out his features, but his jerky movements as he drags his hands through his hair gives the distinct impression that he's upset about something.

"I know we're just friends," he says, taking a step forward. I can smell the alcohol on him, but he seems steady enough on his feet, so I'd guess he's tipsy but not *drunk*. My stomach knots at his words, and I brace myself for whatever might come next. "But could you tell me what it is about Alex? Like, why him but not me? Is it just because you haven't had him yet? He's kind of fun and flirty, that's it, right?" he rambles.

"Whoa, Alex?" I ask. "What are you talking about?"

"You were flirting with him. It's okay, you can flirt with him, I just thought this would be a good learning experience for me, to know what I could do differently with other men in the future." A slight quiver in his voice belies his otherwise calm tone.

"Oh, Elijah," I say his name delicately, reaching out for him before I can think better of it. My hand lands on his waist, and I pull him a little closer so I can finally see his face in the dim light of the room. I brush my thumb over his cheek and look into his eyes, searching for the right way to explain it. "It's not about you."

He snorts a laugh and starts to pull away, but I tighten my grip on his hip.

"Come on, Pax. I may be awkward and in-experienced, but even I know the whole *it's not you, it's me* thing is bullshit."

I've never heard him swear before, and it catches me off guard. He tries to pull away again and I grit my teeth in irritation.

"Will you wait one goddamn minute and

let me explain?" I snap, and that stills him. "I don't do relationships. You heard my friends last weekend; I'm a slut. I fuck anything that moves. You deserve better than that."

"That's all? You think I deserve more than you're willing to give?"

"Damn right you deserve more," I say. "You should be with someone who knows how to do all the hearts and flowers bullshit, who will take you on a proper date and woo you. You don't want to waste your time with me, Einstein, you really don't." The words are like glass on my tongue, but they have to be said.

"I can do casual," he says.

"What?"

He shrugs and moves closer. "We're adults; it's no big deal," he reasons, leaning closer until I can practically taste the sweet smell of liquor on his breath, my heart beating faster as I resist the urge to reach out for him. "It doesn't have to be complicated," he goes on, pressing me into the door with his body against mine, small but somehow commanding in this moment. I shouldn't want him, but *fuck,* he's not making it easy. My breath hitches, and heat flares in his eyes. "We're nothing more than atoms crashing into each other."

And then we do crash into each other. His mouth claiming mine in a bruising kiss, his tongue sweeping past my lips to slide against mine. The timid man I kissed a few weeks ago is gone. There's no awkward fumbling or shaky hands clutching the front of my shirt. Elijah's arms loop around my neck, his hips pressed to mine as he grazes his teeth against my bottom lip before licking into my mouth again. A moan falls from my mouth into his, and I seal our lips more firmly together, digging my fingers into his hips to keep him in place.

The hard outline or our cocks press together, sending sparks of electricity up my spine. It's all I can do not to throw him down on the bed and rut against him until we're both sticky with sweat and cum, just like before.

Some distant part of my brain sounds the warning bells, telling me this is a bad idea, but I'm not sure I could give less of a fuck right now about right and wrong, smart or stupid; all I can think about is the smooth feeling of Elijah's skin as I slip my hands under his shirt and the wet slide of his tongue against mine.

The distant sound of chatter from the party is drowned out by our harsh, rasping breaths and the quiet sounds of pleasure that Elijah makes as he rubs against me. Goosebumps form in the wake of my fingers as I run them up the curve of his spine.

"Oh god, Pax," he breathes against my lips, his words sounding like a prayer. "Please," he whimpers as I drag my teeth along his jaw.

"Please, what?" I murmur, sucking at the soft skin of his throat, feeling his pulse thunder against my tongue.

"I don't know," he pants, twisting his fingers in the front of my shirt, still thrusting against me in a clumsy, desperate sort of way that has my cock impossibly hard, my underwear growing sticky with precum. "God, I don't think I've ever thought of all the things two people can do together. Like, what we did before? I never knew people did that," he confesses.

"What have you thought of?" I ask with interest, guiding him backward toward the bed he'd been lying on when I first came in.

"Just the basic stuff," he answers, a tremble in his voice as I push his blazer off and then guide his shirt over his head, exposing the pale, creamy skin of his torso to the moonlight.

"Like?" I prompt, mostly to hear filthy words on his tongue.

"Like, um, blow...blowjobs," he stumbles over the word and then rushes it out. I can't tell in the dark, but I'd put money on his cheeks being a bright shade of red right now.

"Mmm," I rumble the sound in my throat as I work the button on his pants open. "Is that what you want, Einstein? You want your cock inside my hot, wet mouth?" I drag my nose along the column of his throat, pulling his zipper down and slipping my hand into his jeans to palm his erection through his boxers. He lets out a strangled whimper, his chest rising and falling against mine with rapid breaths. "You want me to suck you and run my tongue all along the head of your cock until you spill your load down my throat?"

He squeezes his eyes closed, and I feel his cock swell in my grasp, his whole body trembling.

"Paxton," he moans my name. "I can't—I'm too close," he pants.

"One day I want to keep you naked for hours, playing with your cock, edging you until you can hardly think straight before I finally make you come. You won't believe how intense it is when you drag it out like that," I tease, still stroking him, but no longer keeping up a constant rhythm so he won't finish too quickly. I know my words are a promise of something that likely won't ever happen, *shouldn't* ever happen, but it's too fucking hot not to fantasize about, even if that's all it can ever be.

"Pax, please," he gasps, burying his face in the crook of my neck. His hot breath fans over my skin.

I stroke him faster, tightening my grasp on his shaft, getting drunk on every shaky breath that hits my flesh, every quiet moan that falls from his lips as he sags against me.

"Tell me you want me to suck your cock," I command, wanting to hear the filthy words on his lips before I get on my knees.

"I want…oh *god*…" he groans.

"Say it," I demand again, slipping my

thumb through the piss flap of his boxers and running it over the head, drenched with his pre-cum, of his cock.

"Suck my cock," he pleads. "Please, Pax, suck my cock."

I drop to my knees and tug his underwear down in a smooth motion, his erection bouncing out and slapping against his stomach. Last time I didn't have much of a chance to look and enjoy, the entire encounter a blur of intense lust. He's not huge, but there's plenty to work with. His shaft is thick, the head slightly curved upward, the tip glistening and red. He threads his fingers through my hair, holding on like his life depends on it as I wrap my lips around the head of his cock for the first time.

"Oh my god, oh my god, *ohmygod*," he chants as I lap at the salty, tangy precum trickling from his slit, my lips sealed around him. His thigh muscles are tense, his balls already tight against his body. I'll be surprised if he makes it more than a few seconds, but that's okay, it's not like we have all night to fool around in his friend's bedroom anyway.

I slowly pull him deeper into my mouth, savoring every inch of his cock as it slides along my tongue, his fingers so tight in my hair my scalp starts to burn, incomprehensible babble falling from his lips. He's so hard I can feel his pounding pulse in the thick veins along his shaft. He's harder than steel, the head of his cock dragging against the roof of my mouth as I stroke the underside with my tongue.

"I can't, oh god, I can't," he warns, yanking my hair.

I suck harder, his cock hitting the back of my throat, and that's all it takes. He starts to pulse in my mouth, spurts of hot seed spraying like a firehose down my throat. I grab onto the globes of his ass, sucking him, keeping him buried deep as I milk every drop of cum from his balls until he starts to soften in my mouth, and I'm forced to release him.

As soon as I let him go, Elijah's legs give out and he collapses onto the bed behind him. I lick my lips, savoring the tangy flavor of his release before crawling onto the bed beside him.

My own cock is still hard and aching, but surprisingly, it's the last thing on my mind as I brush Elijah's sweaty hair off his face and wait for him to catch his breath.

"Experiments are exciting, even if they end up blowing up in your face in the end," he says after a few minutes, his eyes flickering to mine before looking away again.

"Is that what this is? An experiment?" I roll the idea around in my head, examining it from all angles. If this isn't a relationship or even a fling, maybe it's safe, at least for a little while.

Elijah shrugs and catches his bottom lip between his teeth. "It can be."

"And what exactly *is* this experiment, Einstein? It's fooling around, not rocket science."

His cheeks tint pink, and his shoulders sag a little. I'm coming to recognize the look of embarrassment, and I wish I could snatch the words back.

"I wish it *was* rocket science, then maybe I'd be good at it."

I want to tell him he seems to be plenty good at it, with a little practice and confidence he won't have a problem blowing anyone's mind between the sheets. But maybe that's exactly how I can help him, by giving him the practice and confidence. At least that's what I reason, and it seems to be good enough to shut up the part of my brain that's panicking.

"Okay, it's an experiment," I agree, and a shy smile spreads across his lips.

"Really?"

"It's not exactly a hardship," I point out. His eyes drop to the bulge in the front of my pants.

"I should, um, return the favor, right?" he asks uncertainly.

"That's generally considered polite in these situations," I agree with amusement. "But why don't we get out of here and go back to your place to finish our leftover Chinese food?" I suggest.

He blinks, looking around the room as if remembering for the first time that we're not at home. The sounds of the party come back into focus.

"Do you think anyone heard me?" he asks, biting his bottom lip.

I snort a laugh. I'm pretty certain someone heard—he was pretty loud after all. But I have a feeling if he knows that, he'll never leave this room again just so he won't have to face anyone out there.

"It's pretty loud out there; I think we're fine," I lie.

He sits up and slides off the bed, and I enjoy the view as he picks up each item of clothing off the floor and puts them back on.

Once we're both decent, we slip out of the bedroom and go in search of Alex to let him know we're leaving. He's in the kitchen, flirting with someone else now, when he notices the two of us, and a sly smile crosses his lips.

"I thought you two left," he says.

"We were um...talking," Elijah stutters, his face going tomato red. If Alex didn't hear us, Elijah would be giving us away right now.

"Talking, huh?" Alex asks, looking between the two of us with a grin. "I hope it was a mutually satisfying *conversation*."

I didn't think it was possible, but Elijah gets even redder.

"Thanks for having us. I'm sure we'll cross paths again," I offer to help take the spotlight off Elijah.

"I hope so," Alex agrees.

CHAPTER 14

Elijah

I don't know what came over me at Alex's, kissing Pax like I did, completely uninhibited and without pause. There's a theory in quantum mechanics that anything that can happen, will happen. That's the only thing I can chalk my behavior up to. But whatever it was that came over me, whether quantum mechanics or pure lust induced insanity, I'm immensely glad it did.

I unlock the door to my apartment, Pax at my back, my heart hammering wildly. What's going to happen when he comes inside? Is this really just about food or is he going to expect more?

Of course he's going to expect more, I scoff at myself. He's experienced; I'm sure to him sex is no big deal. It shouldn't be a big deal. It's nothing more than simple biology, but it's still a bit intimidating.

Once we're inside, Pax skirts around me and heads right for my refrigerator, pulling out the cartons of uneaten Chinese food.

"I'm starving. I don't know what I was thinking deciding to skip dinner earlier," he says, bringing the cartons over to the couch like I did earlier, not bothering to reheat them.

I take the carton he offers me and slide down onto the couch. I can't stop replaying what happened earlier, wondering if he meant it when he said we could keep doing this or if he's going to say it was a mistake again.

I eat a few bites of my chicken fried rice, eyeing his sweet and sour chicken with interest.

"You want a piece?" he offers, holding his fork out with half piece of chicken on it, the other half already bitten off. I eye it uneasily, and he rolls his eyes at me. "We're having sex; sharing a bite of chicken isn't that big of a deal."

"Technically, we're not having sex," I argue, reaching out and pulling the piece of chicken off his fork and popping it into my mouth anyway.

"Technically, we're making each other come," Pax corrects, mimicking my argument. "Fucking isn't the only way to have sex. I had a boyfriend who had never done anal and didn't want to. Trust me, we still had plenty of sex."

"A boyfriend?" I repeat. Did he *just* tell me like an hour ago that he doesn't date? Or did he only mean he wouldn't ever want to date me?

"Back in college," he explains. "It didn't end so well. One of the many reasons I know I'm not cut out to be anyone's boyfriend."

"Oh." I take another bite of my rice, chewing it more slowly than necessary while I try to think of a more intelligent response than *oh*.

An awkward silence stretches between us for several long seconds before Pax breaks it.

"If you've changed your mind about the casual thing, it's cool."

"No," I say quickly, nearly dropping my fork in my rush to respond. "No, I haven't changed my mind."

He looks skeptical as he picks at his food, seeming less interested in it now than he was before.

"These are all your firsts, Einstein. That's special for a lot of people. You might regret this down the road, once things have fizzled out between us."

"Listen, it's not just about you not wanting a boyfriend. I don't know the first thing about dating, and at this point, I need to focus on school, not on trying to figure that kind of thing out. This is perfect. I can finally enjoy the things I've missed out on without it getting complicated."

"You're sure?" he checks once more. A smile twitches on my lips, and I set my food carton on the coffee table, reaching over and taking his out of his hand and doing the same. Then, summoning that lusty, shameless quantum mechanics version of Elijah, I climb onto Pax's lap.

His worried expression slowly morphs into a soft smile, his hands coming to rest on my hips. His fingers dig into my waist before he slips his hands up the back of my shirt. I push my glasses up my nose, gather my courage, and press my lips to his. His mouth is pliant under mine, yielding easily, falling into a rhythm as I suck his bottom lip between mine and then slip my tongue inside.

A moan rumbles from his chest against mine, his cock growing hard, pressing against me through our jeans. I wiggle against the solid bulge, and he makes another deep sound against my lips. A powerful feeling surges through me, and I understand for the first time what Theo meant when he told me once that he never felt sexier than when he's on his knees for a guy. I get it, and I want it so badly. I want to drive Pax crazy. I want to make him feel so good he forgets everyone else in the world even exists.

But I'm not sure I should attempt to reciprocate in the same way until I've had the chance to do a little research—so I know what I'm doing. In the meantime, maybe there's something else I can do?

I move my hands from where they're looped around his neck and slide them down to his chest, my heart beating faster as nerves dance along my skin. Our lips keep moving against each other, hot and wet, my pulse roaring in my ears so loudly it nearly drowns out the small sounds of pleasure that are muffled by our kiss. Even after what Pax did at Alex's, I'm so hard my cock is throbbing painfully against my zipper.

I move my hand downward little by little, trembling the closer I get to my goal. Through his shirt I can feel the heat of his skin, and it turns my own body temperature up several degrees until I feel like I might burst into flames at any moment.

When my fingertips graze the rough fabric of his jeans, my heart jumps into my throat. I know we've been naked together already, but so far, Pax has been the one taking the lead. He was in charge of making it good; I'm not so sure I'm up to the task. I want to try though. I want to be the one who makes him shake and groan and sweat and cum. The thought spikes my temperature another few degrees, my cock pulsing out wet, sticky precum.

With shaky fingers, I undo the button of his jeans and drag the zipper down. His cock presses forward, no longer trapped behind the unforgiving material, his boxers tented by his arousal. I cup my hand around him through his underwear, feeling the heat just like last time. My memory didn't do him much justice, his cock so big I don't know if I could hold it all in even two hands. How this thing is ever supposed to fit inside any part of me seems like a feat of engineering I should really take some time to understand the mechanics of.

Pax groans again, pulling his mouth away

from mine and tilting his head back against the couch, his eyes closed and his lips damp and parted as he lets out another gasp, my hand moving up and down his shaft, testing different amounts of pressure to see what result they yield. I wasn't wrong, it seems; there's certainly an experimental aspect to sex I hadn't expected before.

Unsatisfied with the feeling of fabric against my palm, I slip my hand past the waistband of his underwear so I can touch him skin to skin.

"Jesus, Elijah," he gasps as I wrap my fingers around the base of his cock and stroke upward. He grabs the back of my neck and pulls me closer again, pressing his forehead to mine as he pants out hot, heavy breaths with each circuit of my hand up and down his length. It occurs to me after a minute that it might feel better if there wasn't *quite* as much friction. I pull my hand out of his underwear and lift it to my mouth, darting my tongue out without giving it a second thought and licking my palm until it's slick with my saliva, and then thrusting it back into his boxers.

The animalistic sound that tears from his throat when I start to jerk him again makes my chest swell with pride. I'm doing it; I'm making him feel good. His hips twitch as he thrusts up into my hand, meeting each of my strokes, his chest rising and falling rapidly with his ragged breaths.

"So good, baby, so fucking good," he praises on a groan.

Beads of sweat trickle down my back, my own breaths just as heavy and broken as his. I can feel the pulse of his heartbeat in his cock, pounding harder with each tug of my hand. Feeling bold, I slip my other hand into his underwear as well, using it to cup his balls, already tight against his body. The proof of his nearing orgasm sends another thrill through my body. He spreads his legs and grunts, biting down on his bottom lip as I roll his balls in my palm.

"I want to make you come so badly," I groan, jerking him faster, bending my face forward into the crook of his neck and licking up a bead of sweat, savoring the salty burst against my tongue. Is that what his cum will taste like? Is it salty or bitter? Will I like the taste? Just the thought of his release filling my mouth makes my own cock pulse and throb. I whimper and suck on his skin, licking and biting as he starts to tremble beneath me.

"Please come," I beg, sounding more desperate than he does. "Please, please, please," I gasp, need building in the pit of my stomach as his erection swells in my hand, growing somehow even stiffer than it was before, a deep growl tearing from his throat as he thrusts harder into my hand. Then, I feel the pulse of his orgasm inside my palm, his warm, sticky release dripping down over my hand as I continue to stroke him. His body shudders as his orgasm wracks him, and I swear I can feel every throb of pleasure deep in the pit of my stomach too, radiating over my aching cock, tightening my balls.

Oh, god.

I groan with a mixture of surprise and embarrassment as my own orgasm rocks me, cum filling my underwear without a single finger on my cock. My head falls against Pax's shoulder as we both ride out our pleasure.

When his cock stops pulsing, I unwrap my hand from around it, his seed dripping from my fingers and down the back of my hand. I don't even think—I lift it to my mouth and drag my tongue through the mess, tasting another man's cum for the first time. It *is* salty, and a little bitter, but not unpleasant. And the heat in his eyes as he watches me lick my hand clean somehow makes it taste even better.

"Fucking hell, Einstein, you've gotta be trying to kill me."

"Does that mean it was good?"

A rough laugh rumbles past his lips. "Better than good."

"Good. I...um...I have to...uh...I'll be right back." I climb off his lap, the cum soaking my underwear already getting cold and uncomfortable, not to mention the tug as it clumps in my pubic hair. Not a winning combination.

"Wait," Pax grabs my arm, his eyes dancing

with amusement and something else, something hot. "Did you come in your pants just from getting me off?" he asks, his voice low and gravelly. My first instinct is to deny it, to try to hide my embarrassment, but the expression on his face changes my mind.

I nod, my face heating. "It was so hot; I couldn't help it," I say, pushing my glasses up my nose as they start to slip.

He groans, grabbing the front of my shirt and yanking me down so he can kiss me one more time, his lips rough and commanding, the kiss fast and hot.

"*You're* hot," he murmurs against my mouth before letting me go.

I'm hot? That can't be right, but I'm not about to argue. Maybe the orgasm scrambled his brain or something.

I shuffle to the bathroom to get myself cleaned up, and when I get back to the living room, he's still there, and it doesn't look like he has any immediate plans to go anywhere—his feet up on the coffee table, a movie cued up on the TV. Warmth floods my body. I don't care how or when this fizzles out, I'm going to enjoy the flame as long as I can.

CHAPTER 15

Elijah

I've read the same sentence in my Solid Mechanics textbook at least three times, and it's not that it was difficult to comprehend. In fact, it was fairly straightforward. The problem is ever since last weekend I can't focus without getting caught up on perfectly innocent phrases like *body forces*. I *know* it means gravitational forces or Lorentz force, but all I can think about is Pax's body on top of mine, the thrust of his hips, the impossible vacuum formed by his lips around my cock, the acceleration of my heart rate when he touches me. *Those* are the body forces I'm currently interested in, and I feel like I'm losing my mind.

I shove my textbook aside and reach for my phone. There are no missed messages from Pax, but we've been in touch all week so I'm not reading into it...at least not much.

In all the chatting we've done this week, he hasn't mentioned what he has in mind for this upcoming weekend, and I haven't asked. In truth, my mind has been entirely focused on the physical aspect of what we might do, and that's something I'm not sure I can ask him at this point without bursting into flames. That doesn't mean *I* haven't thought about it all on my own though.

I've spent loooong nights thinking of almost nothing else. The problem is, I'm still a bit in the dark about what kinds of things men do together, aside from the obvious. Are there more things like we did the first night that I've never thought of? Maybe it seems like a stupid question, even for a virgin, and Theo *has* always told me porn could be educational, so it's really my own fault for being so clueless. I tried to enjoy porn. When I was a teenager, most of my peers, including Theo, talked of little else. But I never found much enjoyment in it. I found the acting to be awkward, and I never could manage to get over the fear of getting caught watching it. Although, knowing my parents, the worst they would've done would've been to have a far too graphic talk with me about safe sex practices. I shudder at the thought.

Even if I don't know some of the more... creative things Pax might want to do with me, I *do* know that I desperately want to try being on the other end of what we did last weekend. My cock tingles at the thought of being on my knees with Pax's erection in my mouth. My heart beats faster, and heat blooms in my stomach as I imagine how he might moan, the way it would feel for his fingers to thread through my hair and tug as his pleasure mounts. I want to make him feel as good as he made me feel...no, I want to make him feel even better. I want to be the best he's ever had. As ludicrous as the desire is, it fills me with a longing so intense, I can hardly breathe.

I'm not delusional; I'm sure I'll be terrible my first time. But maybe if I could find some way to practice or get some tips beforehand, it would help. I click to open my internet browser and type in "tips for giving a blowjob". I consider for a moment whether blowjob is one word or two, before deciding it shouldn't matter and pressing the enter button to initiate the search. I'm hit with a wealth of articles and what appear to be porn. Feeling a little intimidated, I almost close the tab and forget the line of thought altogether. It's probably not the kind of thing you can learn by reading anyway. But the title of an article grabs my attention and keeps me from chickening out—*Blow His Mind: Ten Easy Tips For The Best Head of His Life.*

"That sounds promising," I murmur to myself, clicking on the article. I read through the list, feeling my despair grow as I wonder how I'm going to be able to do so many different things at once—suck, swallow so I don't gag, flick my tongue along his tip, use my hand to cup his balls...it's like the Bop It game from hell.

At the end of the article, there's a video of an extremely peppy girl going over the same instructions written in the article, but this time there are props. No, not a penis, thankfully. She holds up a banana, declaring it an excellent way to practice before you're ready for the real thing.

I glance over at the bunch of ripe bananas on the counter and eye them cautiously. It almost feels like I'm on some kind of prank show where as soon as I start practicing fellating a banana, someone's going to pop out with a camera. I shudder at the thought, glancing around my tiny apartment with paranoia to assure myself that no one's here, and no one will know if I practice on a banana. Well, Pax might know, but that'll be because I'll be giving him *the best head of his life*, if the article is to be believed. With a steely resolve, I reach for one of the bananas and grasp it in my hand.

"I can totally do this," I say out loud into the empty apartment, feeling no more stupid about that than about the fact that I'm about to get to third base with a piece of fruit.

Propping my phone up so I can watch it hands free, I start the video over, this time with my own prop at the ready.

"What most people don't realize is that a great blowjob starts before it's even in your mouth. Never underestimate the power of teasing before you go in for the kill," she advises and then proceeds to demonstrate running her tongue along the fruit, using different speeds, pressure, and strokes.

Feeling like a complete idiot, I flick my

tongue out and run it along the tip of the banana. "This is pointless." I stop the video and put the banana down. My phone vibrates in my hand as I close out of the website, a text from Pax popping up along the top.

> **Pax:** Hey Nerdlet. How's it going?
> **Elijah:** Trying to study

It's not a *complete* lie. I *was* trying to study before I got distracted by the idea of learning how to give a blowjob.

> **Pax:** Video chat me?

That's a new request. My stomach flutters, and my cheeks heat. I wonder why he wants to video chat, like is this a phone sex kind of thing? Do I want to do it if it is? Stupid question. If it's a Pax-sex thing I'm pretty sure I could be talked into it, and I really don't want to think much harder about that.

> **Elijah:** Ok

My phone starts to ring a second later with a video call. I hit the accept button, and Pax's face fills my screen. It looks like he's lying in a hotel bed, the sheets that generic white. A slow smile spreads over his lips, and my stomach flutters.

"Hey, Einstein."

"Hi," I say.

"I'm bored and lonely. Hope you don't mind me calling."

"No, I don't mind." He's bored and lonely, and I was his first thought to call? "I would've thought you'd be used to the boredom of hotel rooms by now. What do you usually do to entertain yourself when you're traveling?"

An uncharacteristically sheepish look crosses his face before he fixes it back into the casual smirk. "Normally, I get company."

"Company?" I repeat and then it hits me. "*Oh*. Well, don't let me stop you," I say with as much nonchalance as I can manage, a nervous laugh bubbling past my lips. I glance over at the banana still sitting a few inches away on the table and feel like a complete idiot. It doesn't matter how many bananas I try to deep throat, I'll never be able to compete with all the experienced men he's used to.

"I'm not in the mood," he says simply, making me think that if he *was* in the mood we wouldn't be chatting right now, he'd be *with* someone else. The thought makes my stomach roil as I force my smile to stay in place. "Elijah." The use of my actual name gives me pause.

"Yeah?"

"We agreed this is casual, but as far as I'm concerned, as long as we're doing whatever this is, it's just between the two of us. You good with that?"

"Yeah," I say again, doing my best not to let my relief show on my face. I glance over at the banana again, wondering if maybe I shouldn't give the practice another shot once we're off the phone.

"What do you keep looking at?"

"Nothing," I lie, my face heating.

Pax arches an eyebrow at me. "Tell me," he cajoles with a smirk.

"It's seriously nothing," I find myself laughing at the lightness of his expression, the playfulness in his tone.

"Then why are you blushing so hard?"

"If I tell you, you'll laugh at me."

His expression turns serious in an instant. "I'll never laugh at you, Einstein."

"Fine, but I warned you." I reach for the banana and hold it in front of the screen. "Before you called, I was...um...practicing ...uh...fellatio."

A laugh bursts from his lips, and I glower at him. "That's it, I'm hanging up on you."

"No, wait." He schools his expression. "That wasn't a laugh; it was a noise of surprise. That was *not* what I thought you were going to say."

"What did you think I was going to say?"

"Honestly, Nerdlet? I have no idea. You surprise me," he says, his tone going soft for a second.

"In a good way?" I check.

"In a very good way," he answers. My face heats again, and I dip my head to hide my smile. "Want to show me?"

Pax

Elijah's sweet smile drops, and his eyes go wide.

"Show you?" he repeats.

"Yeah." My voice drops an octave, my cock already hardening at the thought of watching him mimic a blowjob on a reasonably phallic object. "Come on, Einstein, show me what you practiced."

I've never seen his face so red as he dips his gaze and laughs nervously. "I didn't get very far into the practice."

"Show me anyway."

He looks back up into the screen, his eyes dancing with nerves and heat all at once. "You won't think I look silly?"

"I can absolutely assure you I won't think it's silly at all." My voice sounds husky even to my ears, my boxers fully tented now with my erection. I reach down to adjust myself, a heavy breath falling from my lips.

"Will you..." he clears his throat. "Will you touch yourself while I do it?"

"Would that turn you on?" I ask, and he nods rapidly, his curls bouncing against his forehead, his eyes full of innocence, the heat in them building. "Show me what you've been practicing," I prompt again.

He sets the phone down, taking a second to adjust it so he's in frame and then adjusts his grasp on the banana. His eyes dart nervously in my direction as he sticks his tongue out and flicks it against the tip of the banana. I groan and that seems to give him a little confidence. The next lick is longer, dragging along the entire length of the banana, and I swear I can feel it on my cock, his sweet little pink tongue and those sinful lips.

"Oh yeah, get it nice and wet with your tongue," I encourage, wrapping my hand around the base of my cock as he continues to lick the fruit enthusiastically. His eyelids flutter closed, and he starts to make happy little noises I don't think he knows he's making. "Oh baby, you're dying for my cock, aren't you?"

I don't expect an answer, but his eyes open, only halfway but he looks right into the camera with a half-lidded gaze. "So bad."

Fucking hell, he has no idea how goddamn tempting he is.

"Oh yeah, get your lips around it, show me how deep you can take it in your mouth."

He obeys, parting his lips and wrapping them around it. He hums around the fruit as he slowly pushes it into his mouth while I work my hand shamelessly over my shaft, my balls bouncing against my thigh with every stroke.

"Fuck, Einstein, get it in there," I moan, and he pulls back, his saliva glistening on the skin of the banana, and then shoves it back in, gagging as it hits the back of his throat. The sound makes my cock jerk in my hand; it's entirely too easy to imagine the feeling of his throat constricting around me as he tries to take too much at once.

"Sorry," he rasps.

"It's so hot," I assure him.

"Is it weird that gagging on it kind of excited me? I was half-hard already because you're touching yourself, but that was like an electric jolt through my whole body."

I gasp, jerking myself harder. "Fuck, Einstein, you may seem innocent, but you're filthy, aren't you?"

"You want me to be filthy?" he asks. From anyone else it might've been simply flirty banter, sexy talk, but from him it's a real question. He wants to know what gets me hot, and fuck if that isn't a huge turn on.

"Yeah, I want you to be filthy," I rumble, precum leaking over my fist, making my hand slick as it flies over my cock. "You're gonna make me come being so fucking filthy and innocent at the same time."

His cheeks flare red again, his lips puffy and damp from sucking on the banana; he looks like a fucking debauched angel, and it's the hottest thing I've seen in my life.

He wraps his lips around the banana again, moaning as he takes it back into his mouth. I watch his Adam's apple bob as he swallows, easing it deeper. My balls draw tight as I imagine the tight heat of his throat engulfing me, the contraction of each swallow dragging my orgasm closer to the surface.

Without warning, my release slams into me, rolling violently through my body, cum spurting over my hand and reaching my chest as I continue to stroke myself through the waves of pleasure, moaning Elijah's name in between unintelligible sounds and a mix of curses and praise.

My eyelids flutter open again, my chest still heaving from the force of my orgasm. On the screen, Elijah's face is flushed, his breathing just as heavy as mine.

"Did you come, Einstein?" I ask. He nods, his curls bouncing and his glasses slipping down his nose. "Show me."

Looking shy and flustered, he brings his hand into the view of the camera, completely drenched with thick globs of his cum. He watches me for several seconds, the wheels turning behind his eyes. Then, a wicked smile forms on his lips and he brings his hand to his mouth, slowly licking himself clean, keeping his eyes trained on mine the entire time. I know we're both remembering last weekend at his apartment when he jerked me off until I nearly had an out of body experience.

"I should probably let you get back to studying, huh?" I say eventually, once a heavy exhaustion starts to settle over my body. "I don't want to be the reason NASA is missing out on a rocket scientist in a few years."

He rolls his eyes, but he looks pleased at the thought. "I'm...um...I'm glad you called."

"Me too, Nerdlet. I'll see you Friday, yeah?"

"Friday," he echoes, the smile still on his lips as the video chat goes dark.

CHAPTER 16

Pax

It's not a date, I assure myself. Before we started fooling around, we went to the arcade; this is no different. Just because I know the sounds he makes when he falls apart doesn't make this any different than two friends hanging out.

I'm not sure I have myself one hundred percent convinced by the time I pull up in front of Elijah's building. I text Elijah to let him know I'm downstairs and notice a missed message from Seph.

> **Seph:** Any hope of seeing our long-lost friend this weekend?
> **Pax:** We had a dinner party 2 weeks ago
> **Seph:** *sniffle* you used to hang out with us EVERY weekend
> **Pax:** *eye roll* dramatic much? Lol. I'm hanging out with Elijah
> **Seph:** Ah yes, your very adorable and sweet friend Elijah
> **Pax:** Don't do that
> **Seph:** Do what? I was just saying, he's cute,

you can't deny that
Pax: You're fishing, knock it off
Seph: Someone's a bit touchy
Pax: Ugh, I'm not touchy
Seph: You like him, just admit it
Pax: He's a good kid. And he's coming outside now, so I've gotta go
Seph: Be nice to him, he seems delicate

Her parting words hit me in the chest, making me feel like a bit of an asshole. She's right. He deserves someone as sweet as he is, and he's stuck with my horny ass. But, as I watch him flounce down the steps of the building and over to the passenger side of my car with a smile on his lips and one of those damn adorable blazers on, I know I'm not going to break things off, even if I should.

"Hey, Nerdlet," I greet him as he climbs into the car. He gives me a shy smile, climbing in and buckling his seatbelt, his gaze darting nervously to mine as he bites his bottom lip. It's not hard to guess that he has no idea how he's supposed to act right now. He should join the club because this is uncharted territory for me too. I've had boyfriends but it's been a while, and I was complete shit at it, and I don't see hookups more than once typically. Elijah and I are in that weird limbo between the two, friends with benefits. The water is murky, and if we're not careful, shit could go sideways fast.

I lean over the center console and kiss him hard and fast, smiling against his lips when he gasps in surprise and grabs onto the front of my shirt. When I pull back, his expression is more relaxed, his smile less shy, simply happy now.

"Ready for this?" I ask putting the car into drive and pulling back out onto the street.

"I don't know because I have no idea where we're going," he points out.

"That's because it's a surprise."

"I hate surprises," he complains. "Most of the time they end up with me getting embarrassed or uncomfortable."

My heart gives a hard squeeze, and I reach over to put my hand over his. "You'll like this surprise, I promise."

Elijah lets out an audible gasp when the observatory comes into view.

"Oh my god, is that where we're going?"

"It is," I confirm with a grin. "You're going to get to look through the big ass telescope and everything."

"This is so cool. Thank you."

He sounds so awed a warm feeling blooms in my chest, glad I clearly made the right choice to bring him here tonight.

Once we park, he launches himself out of the car, stumbling in his excitement and catching himself on the door at the last minute, his glasses nearly falling right off his face. I bite the inside of my cheek against the laugh the threatens. I round the car and throw an arm over his shoulders. He looks up at me, a deep blush spreading over his cheeks, a look of surprise in his eyes, and the warmth in my chest intensifies. I put a hand in the center of my chest and rub it, hoping to make the unsettling sensation dissipate.

I paid for a private tour ahead of time, so our guide, Tom, greets us as we walk inside. Elijah's normal social nerves are nowhere to be seen as he becomes fast friends with Tom, eagerly discussing the equipment in the observatory and the process for mapping new star systems. I feel a bit like a moron listening to them talk, but his excitement is definitely catching, and I find myself eager to look through the giant telescope as well.

"This is so incredible," Elijah says breathlessly. "Pax, you have to see this." He waves me over, and I take up his former position to look through the telescope. He's right; it's unbelievable. An overwhelming sense of...*smallness* washes over me.

"Makes you feel a bit insignificant, doesn't it?" I muse.

He chuckles beside me. "It really does."

I step back and give him another chance to look. I get the feeling he'd happily spend all night looking into the stars, and I'm more than content to sit here with him and just soak up his joy. Tom leaves us after a few minutes, telling us to spend as long as we'd like and come find him if we have any questions.

"This is amazing. Thank you so much for bringing me here," Elijah says once we're alone. Without looking away from the telescope, he reaches over and laces his fingers through mine. It almost seems like an unconscious gesture, but it stokes the feeling in my chest anyway.

"You're welcome. I figured this would be right up your alley."

"It really is," he agrees. "When I was young, I had this dinky telescope I'd set up in my backyard on clear nights to look up at the stars. I think I got it for one of my birthdays; it was my favorite thing I owned. But *this* is so much better."

"What made you want to be a rocket scientist?" I ask.

"Wow, hard question," he says with a small laugh. "I can't remember a time I didn't want to design rockets. It's like an immutable law of the universe—I want to understand everything there is to know about engineering and physics so I can make something that can go where I never will. I want to leave my mark in the stars. I want to be a footnote in history in the distant future when they're talking about how we got to the point of colonizing other planets. I want to be part of something so much bigger than me."

There's so much passion in him as he talks about his dreams that it nearly suffocates me, the feeling in my chest becoming too much to bear.

Elijah's hot, that's indisputable, but right now, glowing with happiness, his hopes and dreams spilling out of him faster than he can form the words, he's the most beautiful man I've ever laid eyes on. I think *not* kissing him right now might go against the very foundation of life itself. So, I don't resist.

He gasps when my lips cover his, the feeling in my chest exploding to fill my entire body as he grasps the front of my shirt in his fingers and melts against me. I wrap my arms around his middle and pull him flush against me, forgetting where we are, forgetting anything exists except Elijah. His mouth is pliant under mine, our lips moving in tandem with the occasional scrape of his teeth against my bottom lip as I swallow his little sounds of pleasure.

"Let's go home," he murmurs when I pull back to catch my breath.

"We don't have to rush, you can enjoy the telescope a little longer."

"Fuck the telescope, take me home," he insists, catching me off guard with the use of a four-letter word that isn't typically part of his vocabulary. He pushes his glasses up his nose and looks up at me, his eyes burning and his cheeks pink. His lips are puffy and wet, parted as he drags in ragged breaths. "Please."

As if I could deny him anything.

"Yeah, Nerdlet, let's go home."

Elijah

I know I'm not supposed to feel anything other than lust for Pax. That's kind of the whole point of our *not complicated* arrangement. But what am I supposed to do when he takes me somewhere so thoughtful and looks at me like I'm *someone*? What am I supposed to do when he kisses me like he doesn't have a choice? If he doesn't want me to fall in love with him, he's doing a really crappy job of keeping that from happening.

I know better than to say any of that out loud, of course.

I glance over and find Pax gripping the steering wheel so tightly his knuckles are white, his face pale even in the dim light from the streetlamps. Maybe he already knows I'm breaking the rules. Did I give myself away somehow?

"Pax." I say his name softly, but it sounds like an explosion in the silence of the car. I reach over and put a hand on his arm, feeling the tension ease under my touch. "Are you okay?"

He lets out a long breath, glancing over at me quickly before looking back at the road. "Sorry, I'm fine. I have a lot on my mind, that's all."

I nod and then clear my throat. "Make a right into the next neighborhood."

"We're still twenty minutes from your apartment."

"I know. Do it anyway."

My heart slams against my ribcage, and I wipe my sweaty palms on my jeans as Pax does as I asked and turns into the next neighborhood.

"Now what, Nerdlet?" he asks with amused curiosity, and I feel like even if the rest of this goes badly, at least I distracted him from whatever was upsetting him for a few minutes.

"Drive."

"You're the boss," he agrees with a laugh.

We weave through the dark subdivision for a minute or so before I spot a dark parking lot beside an unlit park.

"There," I say, pointing at it. "Park there."

He glances over at me with a raised eyebrow but turns into the parking lot without question. He pulls into a spot in the darkest corner and puts the car into park, turning to me with a wolfish grin.

"Now what, Nerdlet?" he asks for a second time.

"Now, I want to...um..." I take a deep breath, wiping my hands on my jeans again and then squaring my shoulders and turning to face him. I can do this. He likes when I say dirty things, so I'm going to say it, and then I'm going to blow his mind...among other things. "I'm going to...suckyourdick."

The words come out in a jumbled rush, but I get them out, and I'm taking that as a win.

Pax makes a sound somewhere between a cough and a laugh, clearly not expecting that answer from me. Feeling bold, I reach over and put my hand over the front of his jeans, feeling his soft bulge through the rough fabric.

His expression changes from amused to heated in an instant, and his cock shifts under my hand as it starts to grow hard. I gasp at the sensation. I wonder what it would feel like if it was in my mouth. What would it be like to wake up beside Pax in the morning and take his soft cock into my mouth, sucking him to full hardness until he wakes up with a deep, rumbling moan. My own cock grows hard at the intimate fantasy.

"I've been fantasizing about your mouth on my cock since our video chat the other day," he says, putting his hand over the top of mine and pressing it down against his now considerably more solid erection.

"Me too," I confess breathlessly, a little intimidated by how big he suddenly feels. I'm not sure why I keep forgetting how...substantial his erection is; it shouldn't keep surprising me like this. "Do I...Um...I read about safe sex and everything..."

"If you want me to wear a condom, I will, but I got tested last week after we decided to keep fooling around. I'm on PrEP too, so you're safe."

"Okay."

I lick my lips and use my free hand to push my hair back off my forehead, and then I reach for his zipper, slowly dragging it down. His boxers tent forward, the outline of his cock somewhat visible through the taut fabric. My erection throbs, nerves and excitement along my skin.

"If I'm bad at it, will you tell me?" I ask, managing to tear my eyes away from the endlessly fascinating appendage to look at his face for a few seconds.

"Easy on the teeth and you'll be fine. It's hard to give a bad blowjob," Pax assures me.

"But I don't want to give you a *not bad* blowjob," I tell him, licking my lips again as I hook my fingers in the waistband of his pants to push them down. He lifts his hips to help me get both his pants and underwear down to his thighs, his cock bouncing free and resting, pointing straight up. "I want to give you the best blowjob you've ever had."

His pupils dilate, and his cock jerks at my words.

"Only one place to start then, Einstein," he purrs, threading his fingers through my hair, guiding my head down until I'm inches from his cock. It looks even bigger up close, thick and veiny, the head glistening with precum.

"You're a *lot* bigger than the banana," I muse, and a deep laugh rumbles from his chest.

"Don't overthink it. Think of me like another form of practice, just do what feels right, and try to have some fun with it. That's the most important thing about going down on someone; no one wants to feel like they're a chore. They want to know their partner is enjoying it as much as they are."

Practice, right, because that is what this is, I remind myself.

Reaching out, I wrap my fingers around the base of his erection. His skin is hot and silky, the hard steel of his erection sending a thrill through me. What would it feel like to have him inside me? Would it hurt or would I like it? I shiver at the thought, my hole fluttering and my insides clenching. Maybe I'll find out eventually, but not tonight.

I lean closer and drag my tongue tentatively along the head of his cock, the salty flavor of his precum settling on my tongue as I lap it up, more forming with each lick, making my erection throb and my whole body heat. My nerves give way to a need so deep it feels like I might actually die if I don't get Pax's cock inside me right this second.

I wrap my lips around the head of his cock and moan around it as the flavor and feeling of my lips stretching around him nearly make me lose my load instantly. Pax's fingers tighten in my hair and he groans too. Taking him deeper into my mouth, the weight of him against my tongue fills me with a deep pleasure I never would have imagined.

Everything I read on the internet scatters from my mind in an instant, replaced by mindless instinct and desperate need. I don't care about breathing or technique or that someone might see us. The only thing that exists is Pax's cock filling my mouth. I lick and suck, taking as much of him as I can manage until I gag. Just like with the banana, it makes me even harder, the feeling tightening my balls and making the pit of my stomach heat and tingle. Pax lets out a deep moan, his hips twitching as I try again, doing my best to swallow this time when he hits the back of my throat.

This time, I manage to take him into my throat without choking. If my mouth wasn't full, I'd cheer with triumph. Instead, I hum happily, drawing back and taking him in all over again. Saliva mixed with his precum drips down my chin as I bob my head, filling my throat with him over and over, gagging occasionally, sometimes on purpose just to feel the jolt of pleasure rush through me again. Pax's thighs tense, I'm guessing with the effort he's making not to thrust up into my mouth. If I could bear the thought of letting him out of my mouth, I'd tell him he can do anything he likes, that I *want* him to.

Pax's grunts and gasps of pleasure fill the car, the smell of sweat thick in the air. He loses his fight against his own body, slamming his hips up to meet my mouth, making my throat ache and my cock throb. I whimper and moan around him. My eyes are watering and my lungs burning, but I never want it to stop. I want to die right here with Pax's cock so deep down my throat I can't breathe.

"Fuck, Elijah, fuck, fuck," he groans, tugging at my hair. "I'm close, I'm so close."

I dig my fingers into his thighs and suck him harder, my sole focus in life having Pax's cum flood my mouth.

"*Elijah*," he growls my name, his cock thickening against my tongue and then the first hot spurt of his release hits the back of my throat. I hum happily, lapping my tongue against the head of his cock to catch the next burst of cum and the next, until his cock stops pulsing and starts to soften between my lips.

I pull back and wipe the back of my hand along my mouth and chin, both damp.

"That was fun; can I do it again soon?" I ask, noticing my voice is raspy and my throat a little sore—totally worth it.

Pax gives a weak chuckle. "I think you killed me so probably not tonight, but trust me, I'll never turn down a blowjob."

"So, it was good?" I check, dipping my gaze to his cock, laying soft against his thigh, my saliva still glistening on it. My own erection pulses in my jeans.

"It was fucking incredible. Now, lean your seat back so I can return the favor."

I hurry to comply, unzipping my pants and wiggling them down as soon as my seat is leaned back. Pax gives me a wicked grin before leaning over and taking me into his mouth.

My eyelids slam closed, oxygen being punched from my lungs as the impossible heat of his mouth engulfs me. I was already close, and there's no way I'm going to last more than a few seconds as his tongue strokes over the underside of my shaft, his lips sealed tightly around me.

"Oh god, oh god, oh god," I whimper, my entire body shaking as I desperately try to breathe and hold still and not come instantly.

His spit trickles down my shaft, over my balls, and pools between my ass cheeks, making my hole twitch. I spread my legs wider, rutting into his mouth as he slides one hand down my thigh, toward my ass.

When he slips a finger between my cheeks, my eyes fly open, a gasp falling from my lips. He doesn't push inside though, just uses the pad of his finger to rub the spit around the outside of my hole. Nerve endings I never realized I had spark and tingle, my balls constricting and my cock twitching against his tongue.

My hands fly to his hair, and my hips jerk to meet his mouth, babbled, incoherent words falling from my lips. The coil of heat in my stomach finally explodes, my cum shooting down his throat with each pulse of my cock, my hole twitching against his finger, adding a whole new level I never knew existed.

When my cock becomes over sensitive from the orgasm, I force my fingers to release his hair, feeling the stiffness in them from how hard I grabbed him.

"Wow," I breathe, and Pax licks his lips.

"Come on, Einstein, let's go back to your place and order something for dinner," he suggests, and I nod sleepily. I don't care where the fuck he takes me at this point. Hell, he can kidnap me for all I care.

CHAPTER 17

Elijah

Leaning back in my chair, I stretch my arms over my head and then push my glasses up my nose. My textbooks lie open, spread out over the table in front of me, notes scattered everywhere. My phone buzzes from somewhere in the mess, and my heart gives a happy jolt. It's Friday night, which means Pax should be getting back into town any minute.

I paw through the mess, finding my phone buried under one of the textbooks, a text from Pax waiting for me.

Pax: You still have any of those dorky t-shirts you used to wear in high school?
Elijah: Um...probably in the back of my drawer. Why?
Pax: Wear it tonight. We're reliving our youth tonight
Elijah: You're going to get someone to tease me behind my back, and I'll go home and cry on your brother's shoulder?
Pax: Aw, come on, Nerdlet, you're breaking my heart with that shit. We're going to do

something fun and dirty.

Elijah: That's absolutely NOT reliving my youth, but I'm on board

Pax: Good. I'll be over in an hour to pick you up

I set my phone down and finish reading the chapter I was working on before the interruption. Although my concentration is significantly compromised now as I wonder what kind of dirty fun he has in mind and what that could possibly have to do with reliving youth.

An hour later the door buzzer sounds. I glance down at my dorky t-shirt that says *math puns are a sine of genius*. It's a little threadbare, but it still fits fine. I'm not even sure why I still have it to be honest. It's the only shirt that survived the purge after my freshman year of college when I decided if I dressed better, people would be less horrible. Spoiler alert, the wardrobe overhaul didn't make a bit of difference.

I hit the buzzer to let Pax up and tug at the hem of my shirt, wondering if I should throw on a blazer over it so it's not quite as bad. But before I can decide, Pax knocks at my door. Taking a deep breath, I pull it open, and a laugh bubbles past my lips as soon as I lay eyes on him. Instead of his typical dress shirt, sleeves rolled up past his forearms, he's wearing a white t-shirt and the leather jacket he always used to wear when he was younger. I remember thinking it looked soft to the touch and wondering what it would feel like under my fingertips as I pressed myself up against him.

It's not only his clothes that are different, his stubble is completely gone, leaving a smooth face in its place, and his hair is styled differently than usual, more like how he would've done it when he was younger.

"Wow, you look..." I can't think of any words to finish that sentence. This exercise has clearly launched me back in time to when I was too tongue-tied to say a single word to Paxton when he was home for the summer.

He steps into my apartment, closing the gap between us and pulling me against him. I brace my hands against his chest, my fingers digging into the buttery soft leather as his lips come within an inch of mine. Our noses brush against each other, his breath bathing my lips as he exhales, his forehead resting against mine.

"You look cute as fuck, Einstein," he murmurs, and then his mouth comes down over mine, his lips warm and soft as he teases mine open and sweeps his tongue inside. Every cell in my body lights up, my cock growing hard.

The kiss ends too soon, I chase his lips as he pulls them away.

"We've gotta go, or we'll be late."

"Late for what?" I ask, already considering how I can convince him to make us late.

"You'll see." He smirks and takes a step

back. "Let's go."

*****

"The drive-in movies?" I say skeptically as we pull in. "How exactly is this reliving our youth? Or did you miraculously grow up in the fifties?"

"You never went to that old drive-in back home? They only opened it in October to screen old horror movies, and it was a prime make-out spot." He waggles his eyebrows.

"This place doesn't even look open." I glance around at the overgrown field surrounding the giant outdoor screen.

"It's not, but that's even better, because it means we have the place to ourselves."

He parks his car in a prime spot near—but not too close—the screen and then reaches into the backseat, pulling out a blanket and something else.

"What's that?"

"A digital projector," he says with a grin. "And I've got *Killer Klowns From Outer Space* and the original *Night of the Living Dead*. What do you say, you up for a horror movie double feature?"

"Halloween *is* next week," I reason. "But what's the blanket for?"

"We're going to sit on the hood of the car. Come on." He tilts his head and climbs out of the car.

I *know* this isn't a date. I *know* we're only

fooling around, and this doesn't mean anything, but as he spreads the blanket out over the hood of the car and then starts setting up the projector, it kind of *feels* like a date.

The movie starts to play, and Pax hops up onto the hood of the car, patting the spot next to him and then quirking his finger to beckon me over.

"I promise, no one from school will catch us out here," he teases, a deep timbre in his voice that sends goosebumps skittering over my skin and need pooling deep inside me. I scramble awkwardly onto the hood of the car, letting him drag me closer once I'm beside him.

I rest my head on his shoulder, the scent of the leather from his coat soothing, the heat from his body seeming to penetrate every layer of clothing between us. Feeling bold and a little bit reckless, I tilt my head to look up at Pax, blinking at him with as much innocence as I can manage—which is a lot, considering I *am* pretty innocent.

"I'm a virgin, so you have to promise to be gentle," I say in a breathy voice. "And swear you won't tell anyone at school."

Pax

Lust shoots straight through me, stroking my cock to full hardness in an instant. A groan rumbles in my chest, and Elijah licks his lips, the absolute perfect embodiment of pure as the driven snow and filthy as hell all at the same time.

"I won't tell anyone, baby; this is just between us," I promise, playing my part in the fantasy we've concocted. I drag my fingers through his hair and tug him in for a kiss. "You know, I've been watching you," I murmur between kisses, licking and nipping at his lips, drinking in every gasp and moan he feeds me.

"You have?" he pants.

"Mmhmm." I drag my tongue along his bottom lip and then tug it between my teeth. His cock is hard against my hip. "When you're in the library bent over those big ass textbooks, sometimes I watch you and imagine what it would be like to drag you back to one of the dark corners and suck you off where no one can see."

"Oh god," he cries out, arching against me.

"Have you noticed me around school, baby?" I purr, slipping a hand under his shirt and slowly pushing it up to expose his belly.

"Yes," he gasps as I dip my head to suck on the pulse point in his throat. "You're the only one I've ever noticed," he confesses in a whisper. "I've wanted you for so long, it's like no one else even exists."

Damn, he's good at this game.

His words settle inside me and ignite a longing in me that's almost too much to bear. I shouldn't, but part of me wishes they were real and not part of a sexy fantasy.

"I've never wanted anyone this badly." I slide my hand down his stomach until I reach the waist of his jeans. Pushing even lower, I cup his erection through his jeans, dragging my tongue along his Adam's apple, feeling the vibration of every sound he tries to keep quiet.

"I want you inside me. Please, I want you so badly," he moans.

My hand stills, my breath catching. I pull back so I can look down at him, flushed and disheveled, his hair wild and his glasses askew.

"We're stopping the game for a second," I say, studying his face as he bites his bottom lip and vibrates with the effort to stay still beneath me. "Is that really what you want, Einstein? Because I'm fine with what we've been doing. And there's more we can do short of penetration."

"I'm sure," he answers, a barely there quiver in his voice. "I want it. I want it *with you*."

My heart swoops, and my cock pulses, the head growing slick with precum as my balls tighten, my entire body taut as a bow.

"We can go back to your place—a bed would be better," I reason.

"No. Please, Pax. I want it here, please." He bucks his hips up, pressing his cock against me and letting his eyelids flutter closed as the color rises in his cheeks. "Please, please."

"Oh, baby, you don't have to beg," I murmur, letting myself slip back into character. It's almost too much otherwise, if it's a game, it's easier to remember that *none* of this is real.

I dip down and press a kiss to his belly as I work his jeans open with trembling fingers, nerves coiling in my stomach. You'd think I was the virgin here. Christ, I can hardly remember my first time. It was with some random guy at a gay bar right off campus my freshman year of college. I was so drunk I could hardly see straight. I'm not sure if I ever got his name or if I was so wasted I forgot it. It wasn't anything to write home about, and that's the last thing I want for Elijah. I need to make this special for him. But here we are in the middle of a field about to fuck on the hood of my car.

"Pax, I want this," he says again as if reading my thoughts.

I scrape my teeth against the skin of his belly, and he squirms and laughs. I glance up at him, his eyes are full of vulnerability and lust, his entire expression the epitome of trust.

"I want *you*," I growl against his skin before dipping my tongue into his belly button and dragging the zipper of his jeans down.

He lifts his hips, and I pull his jeans and boxers down just to the middle of his thighs. I don't think anyone will come by here in the middle of the night like this, but just in case, we'd better be able to get dressed fast. I take off my thick leather jacket and toss it aside.

His cock rests against his stomach, hard as hell, a strand of precum leaking down onto his skin. I lick him from base to tip, getting drunk on the salty flavor of his flesh and the feeling of his arousal against my tongue.

"When we're back at school on Monday, would you be mad if I found somewhere private to suck you off?" I ask, taking the base of his cock in my fist and rubbing the head against my lips, dipping my tongue out to lap at him.

"Yes," he groans. "I mean, no. I mean…oh my god, please just…" he lets out a low keening sound, and I smile to myself.

"If you want my cock inside you, I'm going to need you on your hands and knees."

As soon as the words leave my mouth, he's scrambling to get into position, albeit a little clumsily with his pants around his thighs. I reach into my back pocket and pull out the packet of lube and the condom I brought with just in case.

He looks sinful as hell, still mostly dressed, his ass on display in the moonlight. I cup one of his ass cheeks, kneading it in my hand as I watch his back rise and fall rapidly with each breath.

"I'm going to use my fingers first to get you ready, okay? All I need you to do is try to relax."

"Okay." He turns his head and looks at me over his shoulder, our eyes locking. "I trust you."

The weight of those words settles on my shoulders, equal parts daunting and empowering. He trusts me not to hurt him, to make his first experience a good one, to take care of him.

Tearing open the packet of lube, I coat my fingers. Elijah lets his head droop between his shoulders, his body still, waiting for me.

"Little cold," I warn before dipping my slicked fingers between his cheeks. He gasps but stays still, trying to widen his legs and failing due to the constriction of his pants.

I spread the lube around his hole, watching each flutter of his breath as he starts to relax. When I ease the first finger inside, he tenses, his whole body going stiff, his inner muscles clamping down hard around the tip of my finger. Fuck, that's going to feel unreal when I'm inside him. My cock throbs in agreement.

"Okay?" I check, wanting to make sure he isn't having second thoughts.

"It feels strange; it kind of burns," he confesses.

"I know," I assure him. "Try to relax for me, and it'll start to feel good."

"Okay." He sounds skeptical, but after a few seconds, his muscles begin to relax. I slip in farther, crooking my finger in search of his prostate, and when he gasps, I smile. "Oh my god, that's..." He trails off with a moan, and my grin widens. I work my finger in and out, dragging it along his prostate with each pass until he's pushing back against me with each thrust, begging for more. Then I add a second finger and start the whole process over again.

With my freehand, I spread his cheeks apart to watch my fingers sink into his hole with each stroke, his hips jerking as gasps and cries tumble from his lips.

"Oh god, oh god, oh god," he pants. "Pax, I'm...I'm..."

I let go of his ass cheek and grab onto his hip to stop his thrusts, and he lets out a frustrated grunt.

"I can finish you like this; is that what you want?" I offer.

"No," he gasps. "More, please, more, more."

A lusty groan vibrates in my throat. There's no way another man exists who's the perfect blend of innocence and lust the way Elijah is.

I slowly ease my fingers out, wiping the excess lube on my jeans before unzipping them and shoving them down around my thighs the same way Elijah's are. I pick up the condom and tear it open.

"Wait," he says, looking at me over his shoulder again. "We don't need it, do we?"

"What?"

"You said you got tested recently, right?" he asks.

"I did, right after the night at Alex's party."

"Right, and you know I'm safe. Can we do it without?"

I look at the condom package in my hand. Never once have I gone without protection. Not with other boyfriends, not when I was a reckless college whore, *never*. I look back at Elijah and find him watching me, lube glistening from between his ass cheeks.

"Fuck it." I toss the condom back down and shuffle forward, grabbing his hips.

Our pants in the way definitely adds a bit of a challenge, but I'm not about to stop now, so I make do, pulling his hips closer and getting myself into position so my cock is pressed against his entrance.

I ease into the impossibly tight heat of his hole. He constricts around me instantly, fighting the invasion as his body tenses. My eyes roll back, the pressure around the head of my cock making my breath catch and my balls tighten. I've always prided myself on my stamina, but I swear to fuck I could go off right now without even trying.

"Take a deep breath, and try to relax," I coax, my voice deep and rough with control. I run my hand under his shirt, along his spine. "I know it's kind of weird, but I promise it gets better."

He huffs out a little laugh and some of the constriction eases. I push forward a few more inches, my muscles trembling as I fight against the urge to slam myself deep inside him and fuck him like a wild animal in heat. I lean forward, pressing my face between his shoulder blades, easing in at a glacial pace, pausing to give him time to adjust every time he tenses.

"Sorry," he murmurs, his breath hitching.

"Shhh, everything's fine, Einstein. If you hate it, tell me, and we can stop."

"Don't stop; it's getting a little better," he says.

"Not a ringing endorsement," I chuckle, and he laughs again, his body relaxing further.

I push forward the final few inches until my hips are flush against his ass, my cock buried to the hilt inside him, and a deep moan rumbles from my chest.

"You feel incredible," I gasp, pressing a kiss between his shoulders and resenting the fabric of his shirt for getting in the way of his skin.

"Do it, Pax. I want to feel what it's like."

"You asked for it," I tease, pressing one last kiss to his back before leaning back and easing out slowly. This time, I don't take my time entering him, I slam forward like I imagined doing the first time, knocking a gasp from his lips and groaning deeply at the unimaginable feeling of fucking him bare, of being the first person to ever touch him like this.

"Yes, yes, yes, oh god, oh Pax," he gasps, his body trembling as he meets each one of my thrusts. The sound of our skin slapping fills the otherwise quiet night, our grunts and moans carrying through the air and echoing through the nearby trees.

I dig my fingers hard into his hips, angling them to make sure I hit his prostate with every thrust. With nothing between us I can feel everything, the heat of his channel, the tug of his rim dragging against my cock with every thrust, the flutter of his inner muscles as his orgasm gets close. He twists his hands in the blanket on the hood of the car, just like he usually does with the front of my shirt.

"You're so sexy...you feel so fucking good," I rumble. "No one has ever felt like this. You're perfect, so goddamn perfect," I babble the praise as I fuck him faster, desperate to feel him fall apart on my cock.

"Pax," he sobs my name, his channel tightening around me again, constricting so hard I see stars, my balls clenching. I slam into him one last time, a roar erupting from me as the pulsing of his orgasm rips my own from me, waves of impossible pleasure washing over me as I fill him with my load of thick, hot cum, shooting it so deep inside him he'll feel it there for days. I moan again, my hips twitching as every drop is milked from my balls, his own gasps and groans growing tired as his body starts to sag. I wrap my arms around him, holding him against me as I ride out the aftershocks of the best orgasm of my entire fucking life.

"Wow," he whispers when I finally ease my hold on him, my body turning to Jell-O as I let my softening cock slip out of him. I drag him back down to lay next to me on the blanket that's now bunched and messy with his cum.

"Good first time?"

"So good I think it's going to skew any future data points I manage to gather on the subject," he jokes, a relaxed smile on his pretty lips. I bristle at the idea of anyone else touching him, but I know that's insane. Like he said, we're nothing but atoms crashing into each other. But I have to admit, I'm starting to wonder if we'll survive the inevitable explosion.

CHAPTER 18

Elijah

I shift in my seat, trying to focus on what the professor is saying rather than the slight ache in my...well, *you know*. It's been three days since Pax took me to the drive-in, and I swear I can *still* feel him inside me. My cock starts to swell at the memory of how good it felt to be stretched and filled by him, to have him so *deep* inside me I could hardly breathe.

I wasn't even sure I would like it before we did it. I wasn't sure it was something I'd *ever* want. But boy was I wrong.

After he dropped me off at home that night, I'd gotten in the shower to wash up and as I gingerly slipped fingers between my cheeks to clean away the lube, I felt some of his cum dripping from my tender hole. It made me so hard I jerked off right there in the shower to the memory of Pax's pulsing cock, his sweaty, shaking body, his deep, animalistic moans.

"You coming?" Alex asks, pulling me out of my very not-school-appropriate thoughts.

"What?" I ask in an embarrassingly raspy voice. I clear my throat, and he laughs.

"Class is over," he says, and I realize he's right: everyone is clearing out.

"Oh, sorry, I was daydreaming," I confess, heat rising in my cheeks.

"Must've been a good one." He smirks, and I blush harder.

I reach under the desk and adjust myself in hopes that no one else will notice my arousal, and then I shove my things into my messenger bag and follow him out of the classroom.

"So, how was it?" he asks once we're outside.

"How was what?"

"The anal sex," he says bluntly, and I sputter to a stop, a gasp of surprise catching in my throat. He keeps walking for a second before realizing I'm no longer beside him, then he looks back and chuckles at me.

"How...how did you know?" I ask in a whisper as I hurry back to his side so no one will overhear this conversation.

"Oh please, you were doing the *my ass hurts* dance all through class." He waves his hand like it's the most obvious thing in the world. "Now spill, how was it?"

"It was..." I run my fingers up and down the strap of my bag, trying to think of the right word to describe that night. I clench my butt just to feel the ache again for a second, to remember what it felt like to trust Pax like that. "It was amazing."

Alex's smile widens. "Yay, I'm so happy for you."

"Thanks," I say with a chuckle.

"Has he rimmed you yet?" he asks, looping his arm through mine and tugging me along toward our next class.

"Um...no?" I'm not entirely sure I know what that is, but it doesn't sound like something we've done.

"Not everyone is into it, but oh my god, it's seriously my favorite thing *ever*," he gushes. "If I could only pick one way to get off the rest of my life, that would be it. Like, if today was my last day on earth, I'd find some big, burly, idiot of a man who has more muscles than brains, you know the type?" I nod, so he goes on. "And I'd ride his face until I died with his tongue buried in my ass."

I choke on another gasp, looking around quickly to see if anyone else heard what he just said. But no one seems to be listening, or if they are, they're not as scandalized by Alex's declaration as I am.

"That's, um, good to know." Honestly, what's a person supposed to say to that?

He sighs happily, a dreamy look coming over his face. "A boy can dream."

When I get home a few hours later, I pull out my textbooks and set myself up at the kitchen table like I always do. But Alex's words keep echoing in my head, making me curious.

I grab my laptop and open it to the same website I looked at before, typing *rimming* into the search bar. And, oh boy...

Elijah: I have a question
Theo: Shoot
Elijah: Should a person get their butthole waxed if they want to get rimmed?
Theo: Funny, Pax, did you steal Elijah's phone?
Elijah: This isn't a joke
Theo: Wait, who do you want to rim you?
Elijah: Just this guy
Theo: Like a boyfriend?
Elijah: Not a boyfriend
Theo: What then?
Elijah: More of an experiment
Theo: With rimming?
Theo: Potentially, yes
Theo: Ooooookay. Yes, get waxed, and I'm going to send you a link for...um...prep
Elijah: What kind of prep? More than waxing?
Theo: Oh, child.

Theo sends me a link, and if anything, it makes the whole prospect seem even more intimidating than it already was. But I *am* a little curious about the whole thing.

Pax

I lay back in my hotel bed, the TV droning in the background. After a long day of schmoozing clients, all I want is something mindless.

My phone vibrates on the nightstand, and I smile as I reach for it.

Einstein: You know what I don't get?
Pax: What's that?

Considering the kid is a literal genius, I'm curious to see where this is going.

Einstein: Rimming

I sputter a laugh.

Pax: Like, the mechanics or...
Einstein: No, I get that. One person licks the other's butthole. It just doesn't seem sexy

It's all too easy to imagine my little Nerdlet on his hands and knees, nervously waiting to feel my tongue against his hole, licking and teasing, opening him up and fucking him until he's a babbling mess. My cock grows hard, tenting my boxers at the thought.

I think he just invented a new way to sext, and my perverted ass is all about it.

Pax: Seems unfair to make a call like that without any empirical evidence
Elijah: Oh, that's true
Pax: Tell you what, when I get home from Texas, we'll have an experiment so you can make an accurate assessment

It takes more than a few seconds for him to respond. I wonder if it's because he's excited by the idea or horrified. I groan and reach into my boxers, wrapping my hand around my hard, thick erection. I never knew the whole inexperienced thing would do it for me, but goddamn if it doesn't.

Elijah: That seems fair
Pax: It's a date ;)

CHAPTER 19

Pax

I toss my suitcase down near my bed and start to strip out of my suit, the airplane smell clinging to me and filling my nose. Usually the first thing on my mind at the end of a long week of traveling is a nap and then going out to get my dick wet. But all I can think about as I head into the bathroom to start the shower is Elijah.

After our text exchange earlier in the week, I invited him to come by tonight for dinner...among other things. My cock starts to swell as my mind fills with images of his ass in the air, his cheeks spread so I can shove my tongue into his hole and make him scream.

I groan, wrapping my hand around the base of my cock and giving it a slow stroke. I can't wait to play with him all night, to show him things he never thought to want, to teach his body exactly how incredible it can feel.

I force myself to release my cock and hurry through the rest of my shower so I'll have time to get dinner started before Elijah shows up. I'm no gourmet chef, but I can grill a mean steak.

Stepping out of the shower, I reach for a towel and wrap it around my waist and then head back into the bedroom. On the bed, my phone flashes with a missed call. Picking it up, I see Theo tried to call while I was in the shower.

I dry off and get dressed in a pair of black sweatpants and a white t-shirt, figuring there's no sense in getting all dressed up for a night in. Besides, the plan is to ditch our clothes as soon as possible.

Then, I grab my phone and head out onto the balcony to light the grill while I give my brother a call back.

"Which one of your slutbag friends is fucking Elijah?" he demands, skipping the greeting all together.

"Excuse me?" I ask, my heart beating faster at the accusation in his tone. Part of me has always thought Theo might have a thing for Elijah, but I pushed that to the back of my mind after the party at Alex's because I'm selfish, and I didn't want to feel bad about taking the thing I wanted most. But the hurt and anger in his voice sends a wave of guilt washing over me.

"Several weeks ago, I had Elijah on the phone, and he was nearly in tears over some asshole who treated him like shit after they fooled around. I was pissed for him, but I figured these things happen, and he was going to learn that eventually. Then, a few days ago he texts me about some kind of experiment or something, he's asking about rimming, and I'm thinking one of your dickhead friends has him talked into some kind of casual, fuck buddy situation. So, I'm asking who it is so I can remove their dick and shove it down their own throat." Theo is practically seething, his anger palpable through the phone, and the guilt twisting in my gut intensifies. Did I trick Elijah? Because I was pretty sure this whole casual situation was his idea. Or did he only agree to it because he knew it was what I wanted?

"Relax, your pet is fine," I assure him, a hint of irritation slipping into my tone.

"You know who it is then?"

"I know who it is," I confirm. "Can I ask you a question, T?"

"What?"

"Are you in love with him?" As soon as the words are out, I want to call them back. I want to hang up the phone before he can answer, because it's one thing to suspect but *knowing* and doing it anyway is going to make me the worst kind of asshole.

Theo sighs, and I can almost hear the anger escaping from him. "I was," he admits.

My heart stutters, and a lump forms in my throat. "Was?"

"Yeah, when we were younger. How could I not be? He's attractive, and once you get past the chronic awkwardness, he's really funny and sweet. I used to have this fantasy that one day

203

he'd look at me and see me as more than his best friend. But it never happened, and eventually I moved on and learned to love him the way he'll let me."

I don't know how to respond. I already knew it, and at least it wasn't my worst fear of him being *still* in love with Elijah, but it does nothing to ease my guilt. How would my brother feel if he ever found out that I've touched and tasted Elijah? That I've been inside him and made him come?

Before I can say anything in return, the buzzer sounds from near my front door.

"Hey, I've got company that just arrived, so I've gotta go," I say, glad to have an out for this conversation.

"Yeah, all right. But you tell whoever your friend is that Elijah is special and doesn't deserve to be treated like some throwaway hookup."

I run my free hand over my forehead, the bitter taste of my transgression filling my mouth.

"I will."

"Thanks. I'll talk to you later."

"Later."

I hang up the phone and shove it into my pocket. The excited lust I was feeling before the phone call is all but ground to dust, but Elijah is still waiting to be let in, and the steaks are still waiting to be cooked, so I push aside the guilt and buzz him in and then open the door to wait for him to come up the stairs.

As soon as Elijah comes into view, the weight lifts from my chest. He meets my eyes as he reaches the top of the stairs, and a shy smile spreads over his lips, a faint blush painting his pale cheeks.

"Hi," he says once he reaches me, shoving his hands into his pants pockets. He's without his signature blazer tonight, instead wearing a pair of holey jeans and a red t-shirt with a slight V-neck. I wonder how much time he spent trying to look like he wasn't trying. He was probably in front of the mirror half the afternoon trying to decide what to wear so he could look like he just threw something on. The thought warms my chest and makes me smile.

I reach out and loop my arm around his waist, dragging him against me and claiming his lips. He lets out a muffled sound of surprise against my mouth but melts into me as I sweep my tongue inside. He twists his fingers in the front of my shirt, and I slip one hand up the back of his, feeling the smooth skin of his back under my fingertips.

"Hi," I say once we part. It takes a second before his eyelids flutter open, his cheeks even pinker now, the blush extending down his throat and disappearing under his shirt. I want to strip him bare and chase that blush everywhere it touches his skin. But first, dinner.

I release my grasp on him, and Elijah stumbles a little before finding his bearings with an embarrassed smile.

"I'm making steak and grilled vegetables, I hope that's okay?" I check as I lead him inside.

"Yeah, that sounds amazing. Definitely better than the ramen I probably would've eaten tonight on my own."

I cringe at the thought of him living off the meager amount of extra money he has from his student loans and make a mental note to find ways to send over food to his place during the week somehow. No wonder he's so skinny.

"Wow, this place is amazing," he says as I lead him to the kitchen so I can prep the veggies and grab the steak to throw on the grill.

"Thanks. It's one of the few things that makes me wish I was home more."

"I can see why."

In the kitchen, I pull out the things I need from the refrigerator, and Elijah slides onto a stool in front of the island.

"I just need to chop up these veggies, and then I can throw everything on the grill. It shouldn't take too long from there. There's beer in the fridge—help yourself if you want one," I offer.

He wrinkles his nose, and my heart trips over its own beat.

"I'm good, thank you."

Elijah

I sit, bouncing my knee while Pax chops vegetables. I wipe my sweaty hands on my jeans and take a deep breath to try to calm my racing heart. We've done a lot of things together, and after what we shared last week, this should be nothing. But for some reason, this feels like the most intimate thing I could let him do to me.

I *did* get waxed on Theo's advice. Well, I got wax and did it myself, because the thought of Paxton spending an extended amount of time looking at such an intimate place was bad enough, I wasn't about to let a complete stranger do it. I also spent an ungodly amount of time in the shower before I came over, making sure I was squeaky clean. Although all the sweating I'm doing right now probably isn't helping.

I push my glasses up my sweaty nose and shift in my seat.

"How, um, how was your week?" I ask, grasping for something so I feel less uncomfortable. Pax looks up from his chopping with a smile on his lips.

"Good, aside from the *endlessly* distracting texts from a certain Nerdlet," he accuses.

"I'm sorry, should I not text you during the week?" I drag my bottom lip between my teeth.

"I like your texts," he says. "Especially the distracting ones."

207

"Oh," I say because I'm not sure how else to respond, but a happy flutter starts deep in my stomach.

We talk about idle things while Pax cooks dinner—my classes, his work, a movie we both want to see. It's peaceful.

When we sit down to eat, my nerves return. I push my food around on my plate, eating a few bites here and there.

"So, I'm curious, how'd the idea of rimming even come up?" Pax asks with a glint in his eye. "Watching some good porn?"

"No, I, um, don't really like porn," I admit. "Alex mentioned it, and I was curious."

"You don't like porn? Like, at all?" he asks, his eyebrows going up. The reaction isn't a surprise; Theo couldn't believe it either. I don't know what's so shocking. I can't be the *only* person in the world who doesn't enjoy porn.

I shrug and shove a bite of steak into my mouth. "It's...uncomfortable. There's no feeling, you know? I mean, I only tried watching it once, and one guy just started pounding the other. It's just skin slapping and grunting—it's kind of gross. I don't think the mechanics of sex excite me all that much. I think it's more the emotion behind it." As soon as the words are out of my mouth, I freeze. I dart my eyes toward Pax to see if he caught my slip up. His face is stoic, his attention focused on spearing a piece of zucchini with his fork. Silence hangs between us for several hundred heartbeats, both of us seeming to avoid the elephant I just dropped in the middle of the room.

"A lot of the time amateur porn is a better bet if you want to see real guys with real feelings for each other," he says eventually, letting the air out of the uncomfortable silence.

"Oh," I say again because *seriously* how am I supposed to respond to that?

I help Pax clear the table once we're finished with dinner. My stomach ties itself in complicated knots.

"Come here, Nerdlet," Pax says, quirking a finger at me to beckon me closer. I step around the counter, and he snags the belt loops of my jeans in his fingers and drags me against him. Tilting his head down, he bumps his nose against mine, a playful smile on his lips.

"Why don't we go to the bedroom?" he suggests, and my breath catches in my throat. I nod mutely, stepping out of his arms and letting him lead me out of the kitchen and down the hall to the bedroom. "Get comfortable on the bed for me," Pax purrs close to my ear, the heat of his body against my back. I look over my shoulder at him, my stomach dancing anxiously, and he gives me a reassuring smile that gives me the courage to do as he asked. I strip my shirt over my head, my pants and underwear go next, and finally my socks.

I'm so nervous my cock is only half hard as

I position myself on Pax's bed, on my hands and knees. The air conditioner kicks on loudly, and I shiver as goosebumps rise on my skin. The bed dips behind me as Pax climbs on, and I tense.

"Relax, Einstein, you know I'm not going to hurt you," he murmurs in a deep, soothing voice. His warm hand comes to rest against my lower back, and I jump.

"Sorry, I know. I'm more worried about the embarrassment than you hurting me."

"You want to lick my asshole first?" he offers.

"Let's see how this goes, and we'll go from there," I answer with a small laugh, my body relaxing a little thanks to Pax's calm tone.

"You have nothing to be worried about, just breathe and enjoy it, okay?"

"We'll see if you say that with your butt-hole on display," I grumble, but take a deep breath and try to relax anyway.

A second hand joins the first, resting on my other butt cheek, carefully spreading them apart. I clench my hole instinctively, dropping my arms down and pressing my face into the pillow to avoid the humiliated feeling of having someone stare at my hole.

"Look at that, so pretty and smooth. Did you get waxed?"

"I did it myself," I tell him. "It hurt."

Pax chuckles. "I bet. For future reference, you don't need to worry so much with me, I'm more of a *come as you are* kind of guy, no additional grooming required."

"Good to know," I mutter into the pillow.

He leans in closer until I can feel the heat of his breath against my entrance, and my cock twitches as it starts to swell to full hardness again.

"So sexy," Pax rumbles, pressing a kiss to my left butt cheek. "Want you so much." The right one gets a kiss too. I let myself sink into the bed a little more, my stomach fluttering at the sweetness of his touch and the words of praise he continues to kiss into my skin.

The first lick catches me off guard, and I squeak. It's so wet as he drags the flat of his tongue from my balls to my hole. As soon as he pulls back, the saliva starts to cool, making me shiver and my hole to twitch, the nerve endings seeming to all spark to life at the same time.

"Oh," I gasp in surprise as he does it again. He digs his fingers into the globes of my butt, the tug causing a slight sting in my hole that only makes his licks feel more intense. He alternates between the wide, flat expanse of his tongue, and the teasing tip. He licks in slow, firm strokes and flickers along the rim of my entrance that make me gasp. Okay, I *totally* see what Alex meant.

My cock sways between my legs, aching as it drips precum onto the bed.

I'm shaking and panting as he works his

tongue in and out of my hole, fucking me with the wet, hot muscle, licking me from the inside. His hands move from my ass to my hips, holding me in place, gripping me tightly as I lose my mind from pleasure.

I twist my fingers around the bed sheets, heat rising from the pit of my stomach as my balls clench, and my hole clenches and unclenches around his tongue against my will. Pax hums and groans as he licks me deeper, faster, like I'm his favorite dessert, and he can't get enough.

I unclench one of my fists from around the sheets and reach for my erection, wrapping my hand around it and letting out a strangled cry. Pax growls out a hungry sound, his teeth scraping against my sensitive rim. I moan, desperately stroking myself, chasing the orgasm that's so close.

Pax shoves his tongue deep inside me again just as my hand strokes over the head of my cock, and I lose it, wailing as my release spurts into my hand, my hole clamping down around his tongue. I push back against his face, shamelessly grinding against it as I ride out wave after wave of my orgasm that seems to go on for an eternity.

When I finally collapse onto the bed, my body rung out of pleasure and my lungs burning as I drag in gulps of oxygen, I hear the sound of Pax's zipper. I don't have the energy to look over my shoulder, but the slapping skin sound of him jerking off is unmistakable. My spent cock twitches as he grunts and groans and then lets out a deep moan. His cum spurts onto my skin in hot ropes, hitting my butt, my lower back, and even between my shoulder blades. I gasp with pleasure, feeling filthy and sexy at the same time.

When Pax lays down next to me, I turn my head and smile at him with a sleepy, satisfied grin. He grabs me and drags me close until I'm pressed against him, seeming unconcerned with the sweat and cum covering my skin. He nuzzles into the crook of my neck and lets out a content sigh.

"Sorry about that," he says.

"Don't be, it was hot. And by the way, I was wrong: I'm a *big* fan of rimming."

"See what happens when you assume?" he teases, nipping at my earlobe.

"I have learned my lesson," I assure him.

He presses a soft kiss to the tip of my nose, making my stomach flutter and my heart beat faster.

This is casual, I scold myself mentally to no avail.

CHAPTER 20

Elijah

I'm leaving campus, Alex chattering beside me as we head for the bus stop. My phone starts to vibrate in my pocket, and a smile spreads over my lips. I'm expecting a text from Pax, but when I pull it out, I see Theo's name lighting up my screen with a call.

"Hello?" It's an odd time of day for Theo to be calling, normally he calls in the evenings because he knows I'm in class during the day. He probably would be too, but I'm guessing his Thanksgiving break just started as well.

"Look to your left," he says, and I immediately do as he says. A few yards down, I see my best friend leaning against a silver car, one hand on his phone, the other shoved in his pocket, a huge smile on his face.

"Who's that?" Alex asks from beside me, following my gaze.

"It's Theo," I answer, hanging up the phone and hurrying in his direction, refusing to be so dorky that I break out into a run because I'm just *that* happy to see my best friend who I've been missing like crazy.

Theo shoves his phone into his pocket as well and clearly has no qualms about not playing it cool, because he breaks into a full-on run, sprinting toward me with his arms wide. We crash into each other with a hug that jostles my glasses askew and nearly knocks the breath out of me. He squeezes me tight, and I hug him back just as hard.

"God, I fucking miss you. Forget school, come back to New York with me." His words are muffled by his face pressed against my shoulder, but I manage to hear them anyway, and I chuckle.

"Why don't *you* forget school and move out here?" I counter, finally releasing him and noticing a few tears on his cheeks that he quickly dashes away with the back of his hands.

"Are you okay?" I ask, concern flooding me.

"Yeah, yeah," he sniffles and waves me off. "Just having a hard time lately and really fucking happy to see my best friend."

Guilt washes over me, and bile rises in my throat as I force a smile. I've been lying to my best friend for over a month now. But I know if I tell him the truth, he's going to be pissed at his brother. He'll never believe that I'm fine with things being casual between me and Pax; he'll think his brother is taking advantage of me.

"What are you even doing here? Did Pax know you were coming?"

"No, it was a last-minute decision. I woke up at like three in the morning and I just...I just wanted to come see you. And, what perfect timing since we both have whole week off for Thanksgiving. So, I got on a plane and here I am."

"Whose car is that?"

"It's a rental," he says. "Have you eaten? I'm starving."

"I could eat," Alex breaks in, popping up from behind me and holding his hand out to Theo. "Hi, I'm Alex."

Theo looks surprised for a second and then grins as he takes Alex in, all energy and flair. His eyes drop to Alex's shirt, which today says *Scientists Do It Periodically* with a periodic table in the background. Theo barks out a laugh and shakes Alex's hand.

"Glad to see my bestie is in good hands."

"Between me and his sexy ass boyf—" I slam a hand over Alex's mouth to stop him from saying something I'll have to dig my way out of. His eyes go wide, clearly realizing he said something he shouldn't have, and Theo eyes us suspiciously.

"I'm sorry, his *what*?" He asks. "Did this dude who was jerking you around finally stop being a dick?"

My cheeks heat, and Alex looks contrite as I pull my hand away from his mouth.

"He's not jerking me around."

Theo's expression grows dark, a frown

marring his usually smiling face as he crosses his arms over his chest.

"I don't like whatever this is. You're going to get hurt."

"How about food? You said you're hungry, right?" I shamelessly grapple to change the subject. "There's a great burger place just up the street."

"Oh my god, that place is to die for, and there are always super-hot guys there," Alex adds helpfully, and Theo's expression finally softens.

"Hot guys?" he repeats.

"Ridiculously hot guys. Like, all the firemen hang out there after their shifts."

"Way to bury the lead; always start with firemen," he scolds. "What are we waiting for?"

Theo throws an arm around my shoulder, and I lean into his embrace as a way of silent apology for lying to him. There's no point in starting a fight between him and Pax when this thing is never going to last anyway.

Alex and Theo get along even better than I expected, loudly checking out every man in the restaurant while we chow down on our burgers. When my phone vibrates in my pocket again, my heart leaps into my throat, and my smile from earlier returns. I pull it out, keeping it under the table while I read the message from Pax.

Pax: Flight just landed, a full week off ahead

of me, and I can't think of anything but you in my bed. Meet me at my place?

My stomach swoops and flutters, heat rising in my cheeks, my cock growing hard. I glance up to make sure Alex and Theo are still distracted before I type back.

Elijah: Ugh, I would but something kind of came up
Pax: What came up?

I finally bring my phone into full view.
"Smile, Theo."
He gives me a huge grin, and I snap a picture, immediately sending it to Pax.
"That for my brother?" he guesses.
"Yup, he's probably still at the airport, but I'm betting he'll get down here as fast as he can to see you."

Pax: Holy shit, Theo's in town?
Elijah: Yup. Meet us at Frankie's if you want
Pax: I'll be there in an hour

"He says about an hour," I let him know.
"Cool. I need to pee," Theo announces, getting up from the table. As soon as he's gone, I turn my attention on Alex.
"Okay, so, here's the deal. You know Pax?"

"Your hottie hookup, yes," Alex nods and makes a motion with his hand for me to go on.

"The thing is, that's Theo's brother."

Alex's eyes go wide, his grin becoming huge. "Holy shit. He doesn't know you're banging his brother?"

I cringe at the crude language.

"No, he doesn't. Please don't tell him."

He mimes zipping and locking his lips, and I let out a relieved breath.

Pax

I toss my bags on the bed and jump into the shower when I get back to the apartment, hurrying through it so I can get over to where Elijah and my brother are hanging out. As I'm stepping out of the shower, my phone pings from its place on the bathroom counter. I reach for it, expecting another text from Elijah, but find one from Bishop instead.

Bishop: Hudson is threatening to send out a search party if you don't send us proof of life ASAP

I chuckle and snap a quick picture, attaching it to a group text for all three of my friends.

Hudson: Without a newspaper, we can't be sure this photo is from today

Bishop: That's true, if you've been kidnapped, your kidnapper may be sending an old photo to keep us from getting suspicious

Seph: I for one am suspicious because our Paxton would NEVER go a whole month without seeing us even once

I grimace, guilt swamping me.

Pax: Sorry guys, I've been busy with work

Hudson: You're always busy with work, dude. I'm betting you've been busy with something a little more fun

Seph: Like that adorable nerd you brought over and then went back to selfishly hoarding all to yourself

Pax: It's not like that

Bishop: Leave him alone, guys. If he doesn't want to talk about it, he doesn't have to

Hudson: Bullshit he doesn't have to

Seph: Tell you what, we'll forgive you if you come out with us tonight AND stay out later than nine

Pax: I can't; my brother just got into town. I'm headed out to meet up with him and Elijah

Hudson: Where? We'll meet you there

I send them the name of the place.

Pax: But seriously guys, my brother is SUPER protective of Elijah, so none of that suggestive shit, ok?

Hudson: So you DON'T want your brother to know you're giving it to his best friend?

Pax: I just told you it's not like that. If you can't behave, don't show up just to cause trouble

Bishop: No trouble, I promise to keep that asshole in line

Hudson: Oh baby, you know I love it when you talk dirty

Seph: Enough with the foreplay already *eyeroll*

Pax: See you guys in a bit

I stride into the bedroom and toss my phone down on the bed so I can get dressed.

*****

Hudson, Bishop, Seph, and I all arrive at the same time. The hard time they were giving me via text continues in person, complaints of how long it's been since I've come around turning into jokes about what must be keeping me so busy.

"I know I've been a shitty friend recently. I promise I'll do better."

"We're going to hold you to that," Hudson warns.

K.M. Neuhold

We all head inside, and Theo jumps up from the table to give me a hug.

"Thanks for taking such good care of Elijah. He's happy, I can tell," he whispers as I squeeze him back.

A mixture of guilt and happiness washes over me. As I let go of my brother, my eyes meet Elijah's, and he gives me one of those shy little smiles that drive me so crazy, his cheeks pinking. It's all I can do to not throw him over my shoulder and carry him back to my place like a caveman.

Releasing Theo from the hug, I introduce him to my friends, and, to my relief, they refrain from any more jokes about me and Elijah.

"Why didn't you tell me you were coming into town?" I ask, taking a seat across the table from Elijah. "Did you know he was coming?"

Elijah shakes his head. "He showed up on campus this afternoon; I couldn't believe it."

"It was a spur of the moment decision," Theo explains, something passing behind his eyes for a fraction of a second before he's back to his easy smile.

"Well, I'm glad you're here," I tell him.

"You know what we should do?" Seph says, suddenly excited.

"Something with tiny birds?" I guess.

"Or a giant bird," she counters. "Thanksgiving at my place. I'll cook for everyone."

"That would be fantastic. Better than the

222

turkey sandwiches Hudson and I were planning on," Bishop says, bumping his shoulder against Hudson's, who nods enthusiastically in agreement.

"Can you make stuffing?" Hudson requests, giving her a boyish grin.

"Of course. It's not Thanksgiving without stuffing."

"This is so great," Theo says. "I'll make an apple pie to bring."

"Yay, this will be so fun," Seph declares, clapping her hands together.

"I'm invited, right?" Alex checks.

"Of course, the more the merrier," she says.

"Awesome, I'll bring cranberry sauce."

I glance over at Elijah who's been quiet during the whole Thanksgiving discussion.

"You'll be there, right, Nerdlet?" I check, stretching my leg out to bump my foot against his under the table. He looks up at me, biting his lip against the smile that threatens to give him away. I dart a glance at Theo out of the corner of my eye, finding his attention on Bishop. I press my foot more firmly against Elijah's just to see the blush rise in his cheeks again. My body heats from even this slight amount of contact, every cell in my body screaming at me to climb over the table if I have to. Anything to get closer to him.

What the hell is wrong with me?

"Yeah, I'll go," he agrees.

"Good."

We end up closing out the restaurant. Seph, Bishop, and Hudson push for us to find a bar that's still open to keep the party going, and Alex is on board with it, but I'm wiped out.

"I'm beat. I think I'm going to head home and get some sleep." I glance over at Elijah, wishing like hell again that I could drag him back to my place with me. It's only been a few weeks, but the fun we get up to on Friday nights is what I look forward to all week. "You coming to crash at my place, T, or what?"

"I think I'll go to Elijah's actually, but let's get together tomorrow and do some brotherly bonding shit."

"You've got it," I agree, giving him one last hug.

As we all part ways, Theo throws his arm over Elijah's shoulder, and more guilt hits me in the pit of the stomach. Elijah glances back at me over his shoulder, and I give him a brief wave and a smile.

CHAPTER 21

Elijah

Theo insists on stopping for snacks on our way back to my apartment, even though we already ate our weight in pizza and garlic bread tonight. He's excited about it, so I don't argue.

When we get back to my place, he dumps the bag of candy and other assorted snacks out on my bed.

"Let's put on our pajamas and stuff our faces with sugar, then you can tell me all about this man of yours, because I need details." He waggles his eyebrows and smiles.

Heat crawls up my neck and over my cheeks. I'm sure I'm bright red. "There's not much to talk about."

"None of that. I *know* there are juicy details, and we're going to talk about them because it's what best friends do, and I *need* some best friend time with you." The hint of desperation behind his otherwise sunny tone stops me from arguing.

"Okay, yeah," I agree, turning around to grab pajamas out of my dresser and getting changed with my back to him.

When I turn back around, he's in a pair of green flannel pajama pants and a Ramones t-shirt that he's had since the seventh grade, complete with a giant hole in the right armpit that he doesn't seem to mind in the slightest. He crawls onto the bed, and I join him, a familiar peace settling over me. There's no pressure or expectations with Theo; he's one of the few people who just lets me *be*. I guess Pax does too, in his own way. He pushes me out of my comfort zone, but only in the best ways.

Theo grabs a bag of Twizzlers and rips it open, offering me one and shoving one between his teeth.

"Let's start with the most important question, what's his dick like?"

I nearly choke on the bite of Twizzler in my mouth, coughing and sputtering with surprise from the bluntness of his question. I am *not* going to describe his brother's dick to him, even if he'll never know it's Pax I'm talking about.

"All the sudden you want to know about... *that*? I thought you weren't on board with me having a casual...whatever."

"Well, I doubt I'm going to talk you out of your casual *whatever*, so I've decided to switch to best friend mode instead of protector mode," he says. "Now, tell me."

"It's nice, I don't know." I shrug, setting my candy down so I don't risk nearly dying again if he asks another *personal* question.

"Oh, come on, how big is it? Is he cut? Does he manscape or is he rocking a jungle of pubic hair?"

"Oh my god," I mutter, praying for a hole to open up and swallow me so I don't have to have this conversation. "I don't know."

"What do you mean you don't know? I thought you two were getting down and dirty?" He cocks his head.

"We are, but I don't know. I don't really want to talk about his...you know."

He sighs. "*Fine.* We don't have to talk about his dick. Is he good in bed at least?"

My face gets hot again, and my heart gives a little flutter, images of Pax flipping through my mind rapidly like a highlight reel, his hands and mouth all over me, his deep voice whispering filthy words in my ear as his body moves against mine.

"Y-yeah," I answer around a dry throat. I clear my throat and try again. "He's *really* good."

Theo reaches over and puts a hand on my knee, giving me a half-smile. "That's something at least," he says with resignation in his voice. "You like him a lot?"

Yes, my mind shouts, but I bite my tongue to keep from saying it out loud. "It's casual," I answer instead.

"And you're okay with that?"

"Yeah, it's not like I have time for a boyfriend anyway. School takes up a lot of time, so this is perfect," I recite the same thing I've been telling myself for weeks now, hoping if I say it enough, I'll believe it.

"I'm glad," he says, giving me another smile, but it doesn't reach his eyes.

"Is everything okay with *you*?"

Theo shoves another Twizzler in his mouth and flops back on the bed, laying his head on my pillow and looking up at the ceiling. I join him, laying down on my back, letting our shoulders touch. This is the same position we were in when we both came out to each other, and when we talked about me leaving to go to CalTech.

"I'm okay," he says. "I was seeing this guy for a little while but that ended, and I guess I started feeling pretty lonely after that."

"How could you be lonely? You've always got a ton of friends around."

"Being lonely and being alone aren't the same thing, E," he points out, scooting a little closer and resting his head on my shoulder.

"It's not?"

"No," he says. "I know we were joking, but I am thinking about trying to transfer to the University of Southern California next year to finish my psych PhD."

"Really? You should. We could get an apartment together," I suggest and then realize that would have to mean either Theo would find out about me and Pax or things would have to end. It'll be ages before Theo moves out here though; I'm sure by then Pax will have found someone a lot more interesting than me.

"We should," he agrees, and then he yawns. "I'm sleepy. Want to finish these snacks tomorrow?"

I chuckle. We didn't even make a dent in them, which is what I expected. "Yeah, let's get some sleep."

Pax

I'm sitting at a coffee shop down the block from my house waiting for Theo. My phone vibrates on the table next to my coffee, and I reach for it to see a text from Elijah.

Einstein: Do you have any idea how awkward it was to have your brother asking me about your dick last night?

Pax: Wait, why would he think you know about my dick?

Einstein: Not YOUR dick specifically, but the dick I'm currently...you know.

Pax: Currently what?

A shit eating grin forms on my lips. God, I love teasing my little Nerdlet, drawing him out of his shell and seeing the filthy side of him he's slowly learning to get comfortable with.

Einstein: You know

Pax: I'm not sure I do. Tell me.
Einstein: Sucking. Touching. Getting off on.
Pax: God, you're so fucking hot
Einstein: Omg, did I just sext? Is that sexting, because I was actually kind of good at it, right?
Pax: Not bad for a first try. We can keep working on it ;)

My brother swishes through the door, and I put my phone aside, holding up a hand to wave him over.

"Oh my god, coffee. Yes." He plops down in the chair opposite of me and swipes my coffee, taking a deep gulp of it.

"Hey, that's mine."

"Yes, but I've loaned you my best friend, so you can share your coffee."

In more ways than he knows.

"Keep that one, I'll get another."

"I feel like we haven't talked in ages. What's new? How's life?" Theo asks as soon as I'm equipped with a new coffee and a couple of muffins for us.

"Good, working, that's about it."

"You're a workaholic," he accuses.

"Guilty," I agree. Although, since Elijah and I started fooling around, my mind has been less on work and more on the weekends, which has been kind of nice. But his point is still valid.

"No boyfriend or anything?" he asks. He

sounds casual, but there's something in his tone that makes me wonder if he's getting suspicious.

"Nope. You know I don't do the whole boyfriend thing. I'm shitty at it. I've cheated on nice guys. I never make enough time for them; in the end they always end up hating me. It's easier to pick up some fun at a bar and keep things simple."

"Mmhmm." He studies me over his coffee for several seconds. "Don't you get lonely?"

The way he says it, I feel like this is less about me and more about him. There's a hint of desperation, just like I saw in his eyes last night.

"We all get lonely sometimes, right? That's where friends come in and family." I hold his gaze for several seconds.

"Yeah," he agrees.

"I'm really glad you came out for Thanksgiving."

"Me too," he agrees with a smile.

CHAPTER 22

Elijah

On Thanksgiving, Pax comes by my place so we can pick up Alex and then all ride over to Seph's together. It's been a fun week hanging out with Theo, the three of us exploring the city and spending time together. But being around Pax and not touching him has been pure torture. It hasn't helped that he's sent me numerous sexy texts every day, making me so horny I can hardly stand it. And I can't do anything about it because Theo's sleeping in my bed with me.

Pax calls when he's outside, and Theo and I go down to meet him. Theo calls shotgun, sliding into the front seat while I get in the back. Pax's eyes, dancing with heat, meet mine through the rearview mirror.

"Hey," he says, his deep gravelly voice managing to make the word sound somehow suggestive. My cheeks heat, and amusement joins the lust in his gaze. My stomach dances with longing, my fingers itching to reach out and touch him. How can I want him this badly? It's like I'm addicted to him on a cellular level. God, it's going to suck when this ends.

"We going to sit here all day or what?" Theo asks impatiently, redirecting Pax's attention away from our staring contest.

We pick up Alex on the way, and he climbs into the backseat beside me with a dish in his hand and a smile on his face.

"This is so exciting. I haven't gotten a Thanksgiving dinner in two years," he says.

"Why not?" I ask.

"Family stuff," he answers with a shrug.

We pull up to a stoplight, and Pax does the rearview mirror thing again. I swear I can almost read his dirty thoughts, he's looking so hard at me, and I can't pretend like I don't like it. Alex elbows me and waggles his eyebrows and then makes a crude gesture with his hand and his mouth that I *think* is supposed to symbolize a blowjob.

My eyes widen, and I dart a quick glance toward Theo, who luckily doesn't seem to be paying attention.

Seph greets us enthusiastically when we arrive, hugging each of us and telling us about how she's been slaving over a hot stove all day. Like last time, she seems to be dressed on theme like a fifties housewife, complete with a frilly apron.

"Come in, come in." She ushers us inside. "I'll show you guys where to put the dishes you brought. Elijah, do you want to go to the kitchen to let Bishop and Hudson know everyone's here now. They said they were getting drinks, but they've been gone for ages, so I think they were just avoiding me giving them any jobs to do."

"Sure."

I walk into the kitchen and stop in my tracks at the sight of Bishop pressed up against the refrigerator by Hudson, who seems to be doing his best to devour Bishop's face. Their hands all over each other, soft sounds of pleasure coming from both of them. To my horror, my cock starts to get hard. I've never been a fan of porn, not finding much appeal in watching other people get sexy together, but something about watching the two of them is definitely doing it for me. Maybe the obvious passion between them? It's not mechanical; it's pure heat.

"What do we have here?" Pax says with amusement from behind me, and Hudson and Bishop ricochet apart like charged electrons.

"Shut the fuck up, dude," Hudson says, wiping his hand over his mouth. Bishop blushes and dips his head but doesn't say anything.

"I wasn't going to say anything," Pax says, holding his hands up and fighting a smile.

"Good, don't." Hudson glares at him.

"Wine, anyone?" Bishop asks, clearly deciding to go with the *pretend like nothing happened* approach.

"I'll have a small glass," I agree, not because I want any but because I want to help him shift the focus off the kiss we just walked in on.

"What's taking you guys so long?" Seph calls.

"We're coming," Hudson calls back, shooting us one last warning glare before skirting around us and walking out of the kitchen.

As soon as he's gone, Bishop's shoulders sag.

"Sorry about that," I say quietly, taking the glass he offers me.

"It's fine. It's better that we were interrupted anyway." He pours another glass and passes it to Pax and then starts on a third, presumably for himself. "I tell myself over and over things will never be different with Hudson, but then the next time he makes a move, I fall for it all over again. It's stupid."

"That doesn't sound stupid," I assure him, feeling awkward about the level of intimacy in this conversation, but trying my best not to show it. Should I reach out and pat his shoulder or something? He just revealed something deeply personal. That means I should do the same so he feels like we're on the same level, right? I glance over at Pax for guidance, and he just looks pissed.

"If he's jerking you around, I'll have a talk with him, tell him to stop being a dick if you want," he offers.

"Oh god, no." Bishop shakes his head quickly. "It's fine. I've known him my whole life; I can handle him. Thank you though."

"Anytime," Pax assures him. "Seriously, say the word and I'll take care of it."

"Thanks, we should get out there before Seph sends in a search party."

The dining room table looks like a center-fold from Martha Stewart, and the food smells mouthwatering.

We all take our seats with Seph at the head of the table.

"I want to thank you all for coming. I'm thankful for great friends both new and old," she glances at each of us. "And I hope you all enjoy dinner."

A chorus of thank yous goes around the table, and we all dig in.

Pax

"Oh my god, I'm never going to eat again," I groan, leaning back in my chair to make room for my now bloated stomach.

"Everything was *so* good, Seph," Theo says, and everyone murmurs in agreement.

"We should all go around the table and say what we're thankful for," Seph suggests and is met with groans. "Shut up, I made dinner; now you all have to do what I say."

"I knew food this good had to be a trap," Hudson complains.

"Hush, Bishop, you start."

Bishop gives a generic response about being thankful for friends and his health. Nothing real. Nothing like what he was saying in the kitchen. The pain in his eyes earlier hit me square in the chest and made me wonder just how well I know my friends. I always suspected there was *something* between the two of them, but it's clearly infinitely more complicated than I ever guessed.

Hudson's answer is just as generic, and then it's my turn. Without my permission, my eyes dart across the table toward Elijah, and my stomach flutters. I want to say that I'm thankful for the way he's reintroduced me to my inner nerd, that I'm thankful for all the firsts he's trusted me with so far and any that might be yet to come, that I'm thankful for whatever time we have together no matter how it will end. I can't say any of that, so instead I paste on a cocky smile.

"I'm thankful for blowjobs."

"Oh, that's a good one," Hudson says. "I'm changing my answer. Fuck friends, I'm thankful for blowjobs too."

Everyone laughs, but Elijah's smile doesn't reach his eyes. We finish going around the table, and I barely bother to listen to anyone else's except for Elijah's, which is short and generic too.

"I'm going to use the bathroom," Elijah says once we're done with giving thanks. I watch him as he walks out of the room.

"I need another drink," I announce, getting up quickly and going after him.

I catch him at the end of the hallway, just outside the bathroom.

"Einstein," I say in nearly a whisper. He glances over his shoulder, surprise in his eyes when he sees me. Grabbing his arm, I drag him into the bathroom and kick the door closed behind us.

Pushing him up against the sink, I thread my fingers through the thick curls of his hair and kiss him. There's nothing but lips and tongue and scorching passion as our mouths meet, my cock growing hard so fast it nearly makes me dizzy. He moans quietly into my mouth, the sound vibrating against my tongue and making me even harder.

"What was that for?" he asks breathlessly, reaching up to fix his glasses once I manage to tear my mouth away from his.

"I'm thankful for *you*," I confess. "I needed you to know."

His eyes widen, and he swallows hard, his Adam's apple bobbing. "You are?"

"Yeah, Nerdlet, I am."

"I'm um...I'm thankful too. For you, I mean."

I smile and press another lingering kiss to his puffy lips.

"I'll see you back out there." I wink at him and slip out of the bathroom to head back to the group.

"Where's your drink?" Alex asks when I return to the dining room.

"Hmm?"

"Your drink," he says again. "You said you were going to get a drink." The question seems innocent enough, but there's a spark of mischief in his eye that tells me it's anything but.

"Oh, right, I forgot it."

"You went to the kitchen for a drink and then forgot the drink?" he presses.

"Yup," I say curtly, turning on my heel and going to the kitchen.

This time when I head back into the dining room, Elijah is there again, helping clear the table with all my friends. He looks relaxed and at home in a way I wouldn't have thought was possible months ago when we first started hanging out. He looks up and smiles at me, my chest filling with that same warmth I felt at the observatory a few weeks ago. Something's happening between us, and I have a feeling it's a hell of a lot more than I bargained for, but I'm nowhere near ready to acknowledge it. As soon as I examine these feelings and give them a name, everything else will fall apart.

CHAPTER 23

Elijah

"Plans with your man this weekend?" Alex asks as we leave our last class for the day. It's been a week since Thanksgiving, and it's been weird ever since Theo went home. He was only here five days, but it made everything about California feel different, more like home.

"He's not really mine," I argue, as much as a reminder to myself as to him. "But he has plans with his other friends this weekend, so I don't have anything going on."

As soon as I say it, I wish I'd lied and told him I've got something fabulous planned. There's no way I can handle another party, especially without Pax there to keep me from freaking out.

"Oh my god, this is perfect. You have to come with me to speed dating tonight."

"Speed dating?" I repeat skeptically. "I didn't even know speed dating was still a thing."

"You'd be surprised. I think people like that it's like retro," he explains. "And I clean up at these things. Nerds are *very* in right now. Hipsters feel like geniuses when they fuck a rocket scientist."

"That's great, but...um...I'm not sure speed dating is really for me. I mean, Pax and I aren't serious, but we *did* say we wouldn't be with anyone else, and even if we hadn't, I don't really *want* anyone else," I ramble, cutting myself off by biting my bottom lip once I'm sure I've gotten my point across.

"You don't have to take anyone home. It's fun to talk and flirt, and there are no expectations at all, so it's pretty low-key."

"I don't know," I say again, grappling for a way to tell him it's a hard no.

"Come on, it'll be *so* much fun. Please, please, please."

I guess it couldn't *hurt*, if there really aren't any expectations. I hope a bunch of guys are ready to be disappointed by the most socially awkward speed date they've ever been on.

"Fine," I sigh.

"Yay, oh my god, this is going to be amazing."

"What do I wear?" I ask, looking down at my usual attire. Pax always seems to like it, but that's no guarantee anyone else will.

"You look perfect just like this," he assures me. "But why don't you come over to my place and help me get ready? I'm just a few blocks away so we can walk if you want."

"Sure," I agree, letting him loop his arm through mine and guide me in the direction of his place.

His apartment is a lot like mine—tiny, crowded with furniture, textbooks and papers everywhere. But he seems to have a flair for decorating I absolutely do not possess. There are paintings on the walls and little decorative pillows on the couch, as well as other little knick-knacks on every surface. It's nice.

"Have a seat, I'll model a few things for you, and you can help me decide." He waves at the bed, and my skin heats at the memory of Pax watching me get changed.

"I don't really know anything about fashion," I warn him. "Which is why I wear pretty much the same thing every day."

"You look hot as fuck in your blazers and jeans."

"I do?" I look down at myself again, trying to see my clothes in a different light and failing.

"Hell yeah. Why do you think you've got that man so sprung on you?" He flings open his dresser and starts pulling stuff out.

"So what?" I ask.

"Sprung," he repeats. "Infatuated, enamored, beguiled, besotted, head over heels, my friend."

I dip my head to hide a smile, warmth spreading over me at his assessment, even if I know he's wrong.

"It's not like that," I argue reluctantly. "We're just...casual."

"It's always casual...until it's not," he says knowingly as he strips his shirt over his head and reaches for a new one to put on.

"What do you mean?" I ask, nerves and excitement fluttering inside me.

"Okay, so sometimes I get bored of only ever reading academic textbooks. I like to relax by reading romance. No judging." He shoots me a warning glare, and I hold my hands in defense.

"I wasn't judging. I've never read any romance, but it's cool if you like to."

"It's amazing; you should try it," he declares. "But anyway, they all start with the main characters being all *this amazing, mind-blowing sex doesn't mean anything,* and by the end of the book they're all schmoopy and in love."

"I'm not sure real life works like that," I point out reluctantly.

"You never know."

"Something tells me that even quantum mechanics theory would have a hard time explaining an eventuality where Paxton falls in love with me." I let out a self-deprecating laugh, my chest feeling a little heavy.

"Well, I'm going to hold out for your Happily Ever After anyway," he decides with a shrug, holding his arms wide so I can take in the first option of his attire. Then, he strips it over his head and reaches for another.

"Why?" I ask.

"Why what?"

"Why are you holding out hope for me?"

"Because we're friends, and that's what friends do," he explains, donning another shirt.

"Oh." I would say more, but a lump of emotion forms in my throat, so I leave it at that and focus on helping him decide on what to wear, because I'm pretty sure that's what friends do.

Pax

A Friday night without Elijah feels wrong. And the fact that it feels wrong is making me more than a little uncomfortable. I pull my phone out to check for any missed messages from him and find none. Does that mean he has something better to do tonight, or is he being thoughtful and leaving me to have time with my friends?

Half the bar is sectioned off for some kind of speed dating event tonight, which means it feels even more crowded than it really is. And loud. And I'm fucking old apparently.

"Since when is speed dating even still a thing?" I grumble, taking a sip from my drink as someone bumps into my from behind.

"It's gotten pretty popular again, actually. I think a lot of people are sick of online dating," Bishop says. "You'd be surprised how many people can show up to an event."

"Hold on, it sounds like you've been to one," Hudson says, narrowing his eyes suspiciously at Bishop, who shrugs.

"Once or twice."

"Once or twice?" he repeats. "What to find a boyfriend or something?"

Bishop's face remains impassive, but the slightest twitch of his cheek gives him away. Not that Hudson sees it, playing right into his hands instead.

"Why not? I'm single."

"Yeah, great," Hudson growls, slamming his empty glass down on the table and going to get another one.

"Not sure if making him jealous on purpose is the best strategy," I advise Bishop once Hudson is gone.

"Agreed," Seph says.

"I'm not *trying* to make him jealous. He has nothing to be jealous *of*. We're friends; I can date who I want. It's not like he hasn't slept with nearly every gay man in the city."

"You could talk to him about how you feel," Seph suggests.

"There's nothing to talk about. Leave it alone."

Hudson returns, and I pull out my phone to check it again.

"Stop looking at your phone." Hudson snatches my phone out of my hand and shoves it into his pocket.

"Hey," I protest.

"Nope, you're done."

"I was just checking—"

"You were looking for an excuse to ditch us early and go crawl into the bed of your favorite new toy."

I bristle, my jaw clenching. "He's not a toy," I grind out between my teeth.

"Wait, is he your boyfriend?" Bishop asks excitedly.

"No, he's not my boyfriend."

"That's good, because he's on a speed date right now," Seph says.

"What?" I whip my head around, and sure enough, on the other side of the partition, seated at one of the many tables with some big, beefy man across from him, is my little Nerdlet. And he's blushing. I clench my jaw so hard I nearly break a tooth. That blush is *mine*; it's not for some random fucking asshole in a bar.

I grunt, putting my drink down with more force than intended, the contents sloshing up over the sides and spilling onto the table.

"What's the big deal? He's not your boyfriend," Hudson says with amusement.

"Shut the fuck up, asshole."

The guy who's with Elijah reaches across the table and brushes his fingers over the back of Elijah's hand.

"Oh, hell no." I make a move to storm over there and rip the dude to fucking shreds, but Bishop's hand on my shoulder stops me.

"You can't go over there; you'll look like a

possessive asshole."

"But—"

"I know," he says, and the sympathy in his eyes lets me know he really *does* know how I'm feeling. "But if he's really not your boyfriend, it's only going to make things weird."

A bell sounds, and the dude gets up from the table, the tension in my body easing a fraction. But the man who takes his seat doesn't seem to be any better. If anything, he's worse because I can tell from a glance that he's exactly Elijah's type. My Nerdlet blushes again, pushing his glasses up his nose as he awkwardly holds his hand out to introduce himself to his date. A small smile forms on my lips in spite of myself. Jesus, how can he be so fucking cute?

A few tables down, I spot Alex, and it starts to make sense what Elijah's doing here. But it doesn't make me feel any better. Even if his friend dragged him to this thing, that doesn't mean he won't meet someone he connects with. I've told him from the start I'm not boyfriend material, but goddamn if Elijah doesn't deserve the best fucking boyfriend in the world. He deserves someone who isn't out of town ninety percent of the time, someone who can offer him more than I can offer.

Even if he doesn't meet that guy tonight, he will eventually. One day he's going to find someone who's everything I'm not, who can give him everything I can. The thought tastes sour in my mouth, my stomach roiling and my heart giving an awful lurch.

"I need to get the hell out of here."

CHAPTER 24

Elijah

"That was fun, right?" Alex says as we leave the speed dating event. "You got a *lot* of numbers." He takes the pieces of paper out of my hand and counts them.

"You can have them. I'm not going to call any of those guys."

"I know because you're totally in lurve with Pax," he gushes. "But it's an ego boost to know all these guys want you too, isn't it?"

"What? I'm not...that's not..." My heart lodges itself in my throat, and I force a laugh. "I don't..."

"It's okay, your secret is safe with me," he assures me, patting my shoulder.

He's wrong. I can't be in love with Pax. Love is *not* casual. Love will leave me with a broken heart.

It's a twenty-minute Uber ride home, and all I can think about is how *not* interested I was in all the guys tonight. Some of them were okay —they were handsome, and some were even pretty smart and interesting. But none of them was Pax. And Alex might be right.

I trudge up the steps to my apartment, trying to think of an excuse to call Pax and beg him to come over after he's done with his friends.

When I reach the landing for the second floor, I stop in my tracks.

"Pax?"

He looks up from his place on the floor, his back resting against my door. He gives me a wry smile, his eyes burning with an intensity I'm not used to seeing from him. He stands up, quickly closing the distance between us, pulling me into his arms. I stumble against him, grabbing the front of his shirt for balance.

"What are you doing here?"

"It turns out I'm a jealous, possessive idiot."

"What?" I scrunch my forehead, trying to make sense of his words.

"Can we go inside?" he asks instead of answering my question.

"Oh, yeah, of course."

He releases me, and I pull my keys out of my pocket. Pax stands close, his breath cascading down the back of my neck as I struggle to get the key into the lock. His hand rests on my hip, his thumb dragging back and forth along the skin just above the waistline of my jeans.

I finally manage to get the door open and stumble inside, my cock hard as steel from the intense energy sizzling between us. Pax is right behind me, shutting the door once he crosses the threshold, then grabbing my hips and pressing me against it, caging me in with his body.

"I saw you at the speed dating thing," he says, his eyes wild and hot like a summer storm as he looks down at me.

"You were speed dating?" I ask, trying to keep my voice even. True, I was too, but the thought of him going there looking for someone else makes me feel sick and angry.

"No, I was at the bar with my friends. I saw *you* speed dating," he clarifies through clenched teeth. I study him for a few seconds, trying to figure out exactly what's happening between us. Is he angry? If he is, I'm fairly certain he doesn't have a right to be, but maybe I don't understand the rules of what we're doing.

"Alex invited me," I explain calmly. "I gave him all the numbers I got after. I didn't want any of them."

Pax lets out a breath, his jaw relaxing. "I already told you I'm being an idiot."

"I don't understand." Now that he seems a little calmer, I reach out and put my hands on his chest, feeling the bunch of his muscles, the rise and fall of each breath.

"I know you aren't mine. But seeing you with those guys made me feel fucking crazy. I've never felt crazy over anyone before, and I don't think I like it." Pax's words are raw, hitting me right in the chest and making me want things I

251

know I shouldn't want.

"Make me yours," I blurt. It's not real, I know that, it's nothing more than words in the heat of the moment. But I want it to be true. I want to belong to him.

"God, I want to fuck you, Einstein," he groans, taking a step closer until my entire back is flat against the door and putting a hand on the back of my neck. His lips hover inches from mine, his body taut with restraint.

"Yes," I moan. "Please, Pax. Please, I want it so bad."

Pax

I groan as my restraint snaps, and I sweep him into my arms, pressing my lips against his. He cries out into my mouth, his arms looping around my neck, his tongue sliding against mine in a hungry, bruising kiss. We grope wildly, tugging at each other's clothes in an effort to get undressed, only breaking the kiss to get our shirts over our heads. I chase his blush with my lips as it spreads down his throat and over his chest.

Before I discard my pants, I snag the *just in case* packet of lube from the pocket. Even before the speed dating incident, something told me I'd end up over here tonight.

With our clothes in a pile on the floor, Elijah turns around and puts his hands against the door, his round, biteable ass offered to me without question.

I step forward, letting my hard, aching cock rest against the swell of his ass cheek as I lick a stripe up his spine before lubing my fingers and spreading his cheeks.

I prep him more quickly than last time, not wasting time teasing while we're both hard and panting. I stretch him with two lubed fingers, sucking and licking the back of his neck and shoulders, savoring the taste of his skin against my tongue.

When I pull my fingers out, he whimpers.

"Shh, I've got you," I murmur against his ear before nipping gently at the lobe. "Turn around."

He does as I say, turning to face me, his whole body flush with arousal, his cock hard and dripping, his eyes glossy with lust. He puts his hands on my chest, curling his fingers against my pecs and swaying toward me.

"You're so sexy."

"That makes two of us, Einstein," I flirt, cupping his jaw and kissing him hard again, unable to get enough of him, unable to quench the burning desire in the pit of my stomach to somehow possess him.

Breaking the kiss, I stoop down and grab the back of his thighs, lifting him against the door again with ease. He makes a sound of surprise, grasping at my shoulders for balance. A deep chuckle rumbles from my throat, ending on a moan as the tip of my cock nudges between his slick cheeks.

"Oh my god, yes," he gasps, wiggling in my arms, attempting to impale himself on my erection.

"Hold still, Nerdlet. You may not weigh much, but if you keep wiggling, I might drop you."

"Then you can fuck me on the floor," he concludes. "I don't care where you do it, just do it."

I drag my tongue along the pulse point in his throat, tasting the salty flavor of his sweat overlaying the sweetness of his skin.

"When did you get such a filthy mouth?"

"Probably when you put your cock in it," he reasons, and I bark out a laugh.

"Jesus, Elijah, you're something else." My heart beats harder, that yearning in the deep inside growing more intense. If fucking him against the door doesn't relieve it, then I may be completely out of my depth.

"Pax," he whines my name, digging his fingers harder into my shoulders, his cock flexing between us as a pearl of clear precum trickles from the slit and rolls down his shaft.

I bite down on the tender flesh of his neck and thrust inside him. Elijah's cry echoes off the walls of the apartment and sets my skin on fire. I watch his face as I slide inside him, the tension followed by his eyes rolling back and his cheeks pinking from pleasure. *Mine*, a voice in the back of my mind chants. Every sigh, every expression, every tense and flutter of his muscles, they all belong to me. I know it's selfish, but I want every part of Elijah for my own, for as long as he'll let me have it.

I soothe his abused flesh with my tongue, filling him with my cock until I'm buried balls deep inside him, his channel hot and so fucking tight around me. It's different than last time. There was something sweet about the night at the makeshift drive-in—this is nothing but heat and feelings I refuse to look to closely at.

He lets his head fall back against the door, the long, elegant column of his throat exposed, his chest rising and falling rapidly with harsh breaths. He clenches his legs around my hips, his hole flexing around me at the same time, dragging a deep moan from my throat as his inner muscles ripple around me.

"Pax." He whimpers my name again. "*Please.*"

"You're so pretty when you beg," I praise, drawing my hips back and slamming them back into him.

I pound into him, pegging his prostate with every thrust, his cock rubbing against my stomach, making my skin sticky with precum. I dig my fingers into his hips, and the thought of claiming bruises on his skin makes my balls tighten. I bury my face in the crook of his neck again, sucking on his skin until I leave a mark and then kissing the spot sweetly while I continue to rut into him, driving us both higher with every flex of my hips.

My name falls from his lips over and over again, sounding like a prayer if it weren't for the filthy gasps and moans that punctuate each utterance.

"Oh god, I'm...I'm...ungh," he cries out, his legs constricting around my hips again, his fingers digging into my shoulders hard enough to leave bruises of their own. His channel pulses around me as he soaks both our skin with his hot, thick release.

I thrust into him faster, harder, deeper, my lungs and muscles burning from the exertion.

"Fuck, Elijah. *Fuck*," I grunt as my balls clench, and my cock starts to throb in time with his, pumping my orgasm deep inside him. The pleasure washes over me in long waves that feel like they'll never end, the beast in my soul soothed for the single moment that Elijah couldn't possibly be anything but mine.

When I can't hold him up any longer, I set him down, my softening cock slipping out of him. He turns, bending to grab his underwear, and in the dim light of the apartment I can see a trickle of my cum running down the back of his thigh. I let out a muffled groan, and Elijah looks at me over his shoulder with a curious expression. But I don't know what to say. How am I supposed to tell him that everything about him drives me absolutely crazy? What am I supposed to say about this gnawing fucking need in the pit of my stomach that fucking him only seems to have made worse?

Instead of saying anything, I stoop down to grab my own clothes, putting them on quickly as silence seems to expand between us until it feels like an infinite void.

"I'd better go," I say once we're dressed. Elijah adjusts his glasses and runs his hands through his wild curls.

"Of course." He clears his throat and walks over to the door to open it. "Thanks for coming, I'll, um...see you later?"

I grunt in response, stopping and pressing a lingering kiss to his cheek before walking out, refusing to allow myself the backward glance I desperately want.

CHAPTER 25

Elijah

I almost ignore my phone when it starts to vibrate on Friday night. My table is even messier than usual, covered in open textbooks and pages of notes. My eyes are burning, and my neck is stiff, but it's still too early to take a break.

Even though Pax left my place abruptly last week, everything has seemed normal since then. We've texted and video chatted, joking and flirting. Well, Pax flirts, I try to keep up.

As soon as it stops vibrating, it starts up again, and I let out an annoyed huff.

"I told you I have to study," I say as soon as I answer.

"I know, but you have to eat, don't you?" Pax says, and I swear I can hear that cocky grin of his through the phone.

"No, I have too much studying to do to eat."

"I'm not taking no for an answer. I promise I won't distract you with sex. I just want to bring some food over and plop my ass down on your couch to get some work of my own done."

My stomach flutters. He wants to come

over, not to fool around but to sit in the same room and both work? Strangely, that feels more intimate than anything else we've done. There's the unspoken implication that he... what? Misses me? Wants to see me even if it means we're both fully clothed the entire time? I don't understand what that means, and I'm not about to ask and make things weird.

"Okay, but seriously, you can't distract me; finals are getting really close, and I need to be prepared."

"I promise," he assures me. "I'll be there in half an hour with some takeout."

"Okay, thank you."

I hang up and bite my lip against the smile that's threatening, mentally scolding the butterflies in my stomach to calm down. Pax and I are friends, and sometimes we fool around. Him coming over just to hang out doesn't change any of that, even if it *is* really thoughtful.

As promised, he shows up half an hour later with burgers from a place down the street. I tilt my head up for a kiss as soon as he steps through the door, and he shakes his head and tsks.

"I promised no distracting sex; is that some kind of test?" he asks suspiciously, and my cheeks warm.

"No, just habit, I guess."

He chuckles and loops an arm around my waist, dropping a quick kiss on my lips.

"I'm just fucking with you, Einstein. I m-starving; let's eat." He stumbles over his words, and I wonder if he was going to say something else.

My stomach growls as the smell of the burgers wafts up to tickle my nose. "I guess I'm pretty hungry too. Thanks for bringing dinner."

"My pleasure."

We sit on the couch and eat our dinner, talking about our week and joking around like we always do. It's nice, and it's more comfortable than I ever thought I'd feel with anyone other than Theo.

Once we're finished eating, I get back to studying, and Pax pulls out his laptop and gets to work on whatever he brought with him.

"Are you going home for Christmas?" Pax asks some time later.

"Huh?" I ask, looking up from my textbook.

"Christmas?" he repeats. "It's in two weeks. I was wondering if you're heading home to Wisconsin to see your parents. I was about to book my plane tickets, and I wanted to see if you'd already booked yours."

"Oh, no, I wasn't planning to go home. My parents are on some humanitarian mission thing in Africa, so there's nothing for me to go home to."

"Of course there's stuff for you to go home to. Theo will be there. You can spend Christmas with my family."

"I don't want to impose," I argue weakly. I haven't been all that excited about the idea of spending Christmas alone, but I wasn't about to invite myself to spend it with the Reynolds.

"Please, you've been Theo's best friend since middle school; you're practically family. In fact, if I show up without you and they all find out you're here all alone for Christmas, I guarantee my parents *and* Theo will all kick my ass."

"That would be a shame because it's a *very* nice ass," I tease, and Pax gives a surprised laugh.

"Holy shit, was that flirting?"

"Maybe." A smile creeps over my lips, a happy little flutter taking up residence in my stomach.

"You'll come for Christmas?" he checks, looking back at his computer.

"Sure, I'll come," I agree. "And now, I'm ready for a study break." I get up from the table, waggling my eyebrows at him.

"I *love* study breaks. It's what I was best at in college."

Pax

I set my laptop aside, and Elijah crawls into my lap, and for the first time all week, the weight that's been living in my chest lifts. After our heated encounter last weekend, I found myself thinking even more about him this week than I have been. It felt like something shifted between us, and I can't put my finger on exactly what it was. Or maybe I'm afraid to put my finger on exactly what it was.

I run my hands up his back, under his shirt, loving the feeling of his smooth skin under my fingertips. He tilts his head down, brushing his lips against mine in a barely there kiss, his nose bumping against mine as his warm breath fans over my lips. Shifting his weight in my lap, he presses himself against my growing erection, and we both gasp quietly.

I need to feel more of him, want to soak up every inch of his body and devour it. Tightening my hold on him, I rise from the couch with Elijah in my arms. He gasps in surprise, and I chuckle as he scrambles to wrap his arms around my neck and his legs around my waist to keep from falling.

"A little warning would've been nice," he complains as I carry him over to the bed.

"Where's the fun in that?" I tease, nipping at his bottom lip and then soothing it with my tongue.

I drop him onto the bed and crawl on top of him, claiming his lips again. Elijah digs his fingers into my biceps and kisses me back with a hunger that sets my insides on fire with need and lust and more of those things I'm not ready to look at too closely. Dragging my fingers through his hair, I kiss him harder, deeper, pouring all those unspoken and undefined feelings into him.

"I swear to god, I'm addicted to you," I murmur against his lips, dipping my tongue into his mouth before he can respond.

For once, I'm not in a hurry to get him out of his clothes, content to taste him and drink in the desperate little sounds he feeds me as he writhes beneath me. I trail my lips along his jaw and down his throat, savoring the flavor of his skin against my tongue.

As I make my way back up to his mouth, he turns his head and lets out a jaw-cracking yawn.

"Sorry, that's not sexy," he apologizes with a chuckle.

"You're fine. Are you tired?"

"I haven't gotten much sleep this week. I've been up late studying every night." He yawns again.

"You should get some sleep." I give him a peck on the forehead and roll off him.

"No, wait," he protests, reaching for me.

"You need a good night's sleep," I tell him, noticing for the first time the dark circles under his eyes.

"I don't want you to leave yet."

Longing wars with reason. The thought of staying, of falling asleep with Elijah in my arms and waking up next to him sounds nice...*too* nice. The lines are blurring rapidly, and I'm certain I'm running out of time to correct course before we go off the rails.

"Just a little while," I compromise, and his

face lights up with a wide smile.

"Thank you." He gets up and wiggles out of his jeans, tossing them into the nearby hamper. He takes off his glasses and sets them on the nightstand before finally peeling back the blanket and climbing back into bed. I stay dressed, lying on top of the blankets, but I *do* open my arms so he can scoot back against me, my body curled around his. He lets out a contented sigh, his whole body relaxing into mine.

"Sleep well, Nerdlet," I murmur, pressing my lips to the back of his neck. He sighs happily, and within five minutes he's fast asleep.

His back rises and falls steadily against my chest with each even breath he takes. I brush his curls off his forehead and drink in the peace of watching him sleep, my chest doing that funny, warm thing again that's getting difficult to ignore.

I reach into my pocket and pull out my phone, typing a message to Bishop, because he's the only one I can imagine not laughing at me for what I'm about to ask.

Pax: What does it mean if you go over to your fuck buddy's house and spend the night working side by side and then instead of having sex you just hold him while he sleeps?
Bishop: You want an honest answer to that?
Pax: I think so. I've been avoiding asking myself this question, and I'm not sure I can run

from it much longer.

Pax: I knew he had to study tonight, and I wanted to see him even if it meant we wouldn't have sex. I just wanted to BE with him.

Bishop: I think it means you're in love with him

Pax: Yeah, that's what I was afraid of

CHAPTER 26

Elijah

There is no darkness, only absence of light. And I'm starting to think there is no loneliness, only absence of Pax. For me, anyway. He's been avoiding me since the night he suggested I come to the Reynolds' for Christmas. He's responded to my texts but only with short, one-word answers. There haven't been any flirting or silly comments, and he hasn't come over or asked to hang out.

My phone vibrates, and I nearly break my neck diving for it.

> **Pax:** Don't forget, our flight is at 7am tomorrow. I'll be over to pick you up at 5:30
> **Elijah:** You still want me to come for Xmas? I wasn't sure

Did that sound snotty? Did I mean it to? Maybe he hasn't meant anything by his absence; I'm sure the end of the year is busy for him with work. Even if he's not all that busy, he doesn't owe me any kind of explanation.

> **Pax:** Why wouldn't I?

Elijah: You tell me.

Okay, that *definitely* sounded snarky.

Elijah: I haven't seen you in two weeks.

Great, that sounds needy instead. *Kill me*

Elijah: Is it because I fell asleep?

I officially need to be banned from texting for the rest of eternity.

Pax: You had finals. I had deals to wrap up before the end of the year. Don't overthink it

Is he right? Have I been driving myself crazy overthinking things when everything is fine between us?

Elijah: Ok, yeah, I'll be ready when you get here in the morning
Pax: Good. Get some sleep. I'll see you in the morning

I don't sleep. I toss and turn all night, going over every second of our last interaction, trying to figure out where I might've gone wrong. By the time the sun starts to peek through my curtains, my eyes feel like sandpaper, and I still don't have any new answers for myself.

I drag myself out of bed and make some coffee, going through the motions of getting dressed like a zombie.

At five thirty on the dot, Pax texts me to let me know he's waiting outside, and I grab my duffle bag full of clothes and head down to meet him. On my way down the steps, I give myself a pep talk about not freaking out if he's as cold and distant in person as he has been via text. *I can be aloof too. I totally can.*

I toss my bag in the backseat and then slide into the passenger side, my resolve to be cool and detached as strong as steel. And then, Pax turns to me with a crooked smile.

"Hey, Nerdlet," he says in a low, smooth voice, leaning over and brushing a kiss against my cheek.

"Hey," I breathe out in a shaky voice. So much for cool and detached.

The flight to Illinois feels long and is just turbulent enough to leave me airsick by the time we land.

Theo picks us up from the airport since his flight got in yesterday. The hug he gives me as soon as we reach each other is exactly what I needed. It's a reminder that whatever happens with Pax, I'll still have my best friend...as long as he doesn't find out what I'm doing.

Pax

The sound of Elijah's laugh from across the room draws my attention. He's on the couch with Theo, both of them laughing and smiling. To anyone else I'm sure he looks exactly like he always has—a little nerdy, a bit shy, cute as hell. The air of innocence about him as he brushes his curls off his forehead and wrinkles his nose at something my brother says hits me square in the chest.

I've been avoiding him like a dipshit for two weeks, and it's been the longest two weeks of my life.

I pull out my phone and type a quick message.

Pax: You know, you've got this cute, innocent vibe going, and now that I know that's a total lie, it kind of gets me weak as fuck

I watch as he reaches into his pocket and pulls out his phone to read the message I sent. The blush that spreads over his cheeks gets my dick hard, which is a bit awkward considering we're in the living room with my entire family. Elijah glances up, and our eyes meet for a fraction of a second, but it's a second I think I could live in for the rest of my life, and that scares the hell out of me. I tear my eyes away from his and swallow hard as my heart attempts to beat right through my chest. The walls feel like they're closing in around me, and I can't drag in a proper breath.

"Are you okay, sweetie?" my mom asks, putting a hand on my shoulder, which only serves to make me feel more claustrophobic.

"I'm fine, just need a little air." I set down my glass of eggnog and stand up. I can feel Elijah's eyes on me as I flee from the living room like a rat from a sinking ship, but I don't let myself look back.

I slip on my shoes and step out onto the icy porch. *Goddamn, do I miss California right now.* I shove my hands into my pockets and hunch my shoulders against the cold. It's not just the weather I miss: everything feels simpler when we're there. Our casual relationship has been working out great, so why the hell do I want things with him that have absolutely nothing to do with sex?

The door opens behind me, and I hold my breath, hoping it's Elijah and hoping it's *not* Elijah at the same time. My head is too fucked up right now, but all I want to do is kiss him and hope it sets the world right on its axis again.

"You okay?" Theo asks.

I don't turn to look at him. I just look out over the pristine blanket of snow covering the front yard.

"I'm fine," I lie.

We stand in silence for a few minutes, the cold nipping at my face and freezing me through to my bones.

"Are you fucking him?" my brother asks bluntly, catching me completely off guard. I finally do glance over at him and see worry and maybe a hint of pain in his expression. I want to lie; Elijah and I agreed no one needed to know about whatever it is we're doing. Theo wanted to rip the head off whoever he thought was taking advantage of his best friend; how's he going to feel knowing it's me? But the longer I look at him, the more sure I am I can't lie to him.

"Yeah."

His jaw ticks, and his eyes darken. I wonder for a second if he's going to haul off and hit me. I wouldn't blame him if he did.

"You are such a fucking asshole," he mutters, shaking his head.

"I know," I agree.

"I'd tell you to stay the hell away from him, but the way he lit up when he got that text from you a few minutes ago, I know it's already way too late for that." He sighs and shakes his head again. "I swear to god if you break his heart, I will fucking kill you."

"I know," I say again.

"He's too good for you," he adds.

"I know," I reply for the third time.

The door opens again, and Elijah peeks his

head out. My frozen body heats at the sight of him, and I know Theo's right: it's too late to get out of this without things getting messy. I fucked up.

"It's freezing out; you guys should come inside before you get frostbite. Also, your mom says dinner is in five minutes."

After dinner, I head up to my bedroom to get a little more space and to try to get my head clear. It feels strange being back here. It's like a time capsule of my youth, nothing out of place since the day I left for college. I wander around the room, picking up random items off the shelves and running my hands over the books stacked there.

"Did I do something?"

I whip my head around at the sound of Elijah's voice to find him standing in the doorway of my childhood bedroom. I set down the Walkman and turn to face him.

"Oh, Einstein," I sigh, waving him in. He steps inside and closes the door behind him. "You didn't do anything. It's all me."

"So, it's not me, it's you?" he asks skeptically.

"It honestly is," I assure him.

"Do you maybe want to tell me exactly what *it* is?" He bites his bottom lip and steps farther into the room, uncertainty in his expression.

My stomach squirms, and my pulse thunders in my ears. My tongue feels too big for my mouth, words nowhere to be found. I think Bishop was right. Here I thought Elijah might not be able to keep things casual, and I'm the one who went and fell in love.

He closes the distance between us until we're chest to chest, his face tilted up toward mine.

"Or," he says, putting his hands on my chest. "We can *not* talk about it."

A relieved breath whooshes out of my lungs, and I wrap my arms around Elijah's waist. "I'm pretty good at not talking."

He chuckles, pressing a kiss to my chin and then another square on my lips. My heart gives a flip, and I tighten my arms around him.

"Hey, Pax." Theo bangs on my door. "Have you seen Elijah?" I grit my teeth. I know *exactly* what he's doing, but I'm not going to call him out on it in front of Elijah.

"Nope," I call out, and Elijah stifles a laugh against my chest.

"If you see him, tell him I have *Christmas Vacation* ready to go and popcorn in the microwave."

"Will do," I answer. I listen as his footsteps disappear down the hall.

Elijah sighs and sags against me for a second.

"I should get down there. I promised him we'd do a Christmas movie marathon."

"All right, let's do it," I agree, pressing a kiss to the top of his head before releasing him from my grasp.

*****

Lying on my back in the dark of my childhood bedroom, my thoughts chase each other around like greyhounds on speed. My conversation with Theo earlier plays on repeat, along with the feelings that swamped me when I looked at Elijah earlier.

There's a light tap on the door that jolts my heart. It could only be one person coming to see me at this time of night, and I consider staying quiet, feigning sleep. But when the door creaks open, the only action that makes sense to my brain is to lift the corner of my blankets to welcome him to me. He shuts the door quietly behind him, a soft click of the lock sounding like thunder in the otherwise silent house. And then he tiptoes across the room to climb in beside me.

His body is warm as he shifts around under the covers, trying to make himself comfortable.

"Is this okay?" he asks in a whisper, and I nod, turning my head and capturing his lips in a brief kiss. My heart gives another one of those damn flutters. There's no denying that I'm head over heels in love with him. Which means it's time to call things off. They've already gone on too long; I think we both know that.

"I was lying in bed thinking about that thing you do with your tongue," he murmurs, pressing closer to me so I can feel his hot, hard cock against my thigh through his pajama pants. "And then I thought, *what am I doing in here all horny and alone when Pax is right across the hall?*"

I groan quietly, capturing his lips again because I can't help myself. I can't break things off on Christmas anyway. It can wait another week. Another week won't hurt anything.

"Oh yeah, the thing with my tongue? You may have to remind me exactly what that is, because I'm drawing a blank," I tease in a husky tone.

"You're so mean," he complains, thrusting against my thigh, his cock flexing.

I drag my hand down his back until I reach his ass, cupping the cheek as I roll onto my side to face him, drawing his entire body closer. "Tell me the thing you like," I demand in a deep rumble.

A breathless sound escapes his throat, settling deep and lighting a fire inside me.

"The thing where you shove your tongue inside me and lick me open so I can...so I can take your cock," he pants, his hips twitching again seemingly involuntarily. "I love the feeling of your fingers digging into my butt cheeks when you spread them open to lick me. I...god, Pax, I want it so bad."

K.M. Neuhold

"You know I'll always give you what you need," I murmur, nuzzling his throat. "Climb up on my face so I can lick you."

"Sit on your face?" he repeats. "What if I suffocate you?"

"Nerdlet, you weigh next to nothing. If you're suffocating me, I can move you off my face."

"Okay, yeah, that sounds kind of hot."

He slips his hands under the covers and wiggles out of his pants, tossing them onto the floor next to the bed. His shirt goes next, joining his pants on the floor. I follow suit, stripping down and chucking my clothes onto the floor. I scoot down the bed a little so Elijah has plenty of space, and then he awkwardly shuffles into position, kneeling over me with his hands braced on the headboard.

I groan, turning my head to one side and sucking a bruise onto the inside of his thigh.

He gasps, widening his legs to bring himself closer to my face, his balls swaying a few inches from my mouth. I drag my tongue along one, and then the other, feeling them tighten against my tongue as I do.

Grabbing onto his firm, round ass cheeks, I push him forward an inch so I can snake my tongue between his cheeks, teasing the rough, textured skin of his entrance. He moans quietly, the faintest sound bouncing off the walls of the bedroom.

I lap at his hole, feeling it soften against my tongue with each stroke. When I work my tongue inside, he cries out.

"Shh," I murmur before licking him again.

"Sorry," he gasps. "Feels so good."

I hum, flicking the tip of my tongue along his rim and then shoving it all the way inside again, opening him for my cock.

Elijah makes muffled noises as his hips start to twitch, grinding himself against my face, taking what he needs from me. So. Fucking. Hot.

I lick him deeper, fucking him with my tongue until he's soft and ready for me. Then, I put my hands on his hips and lift him off my face.

He makes a disgruntled sound in the back of his throat, and I chuckle.

"Shh," I say again. "I've got something else for you," I assure him with a smirk as I move him down my body and deposit him over my aching erection.

"Yes," he gasps, catching on to where this is going.

I hold my cock steady by the base, and Elijah sinks down onto it at a glacially slow pace, engulfing me half an inch at a time until I'm sure I'll go insane from waiting. When his ass rests against my thighs, his cock pressed against my stomach, I wrap my arms around him, running my hands up and down his spine. He dips his head and buries his face in the crook of my neck, holding his body still as he clenches and unclenches himself around my cock, quiet gasps puffing hot breath against my skin.

He circles his hips slowly, riding my cock like he has all the time in the world. He throws his head back in the moonlight, his face the exquisite combination of pleasure and pain as he bites down on his bottom lip, his eyebrows pulled together like he can't believe anything could feel this good.

Our orgasms roll over us in more of a surprise wave than an explosion, going on and on as we continue to rock together, sharing breath and dragging our mouths against each other's in the best approximation of a kiss we can manage as pleasure drags us under.

I hold him close, staying inside of him as long as I can manage before my softening cock slips out. Then, I roll him onto the bed and press a kiss to his temple.

"There's this idea in string theory that there are infinite parallel universes with infinite possibilities," he says, settling closer to me, his soft cock, still wet with his cum, pressing against my thigh as he hitches a leg over mine and nestles his head onto my chest. He lets out a content sigh, his whole body relaxing into me. "I hope we're doing this in every single one of them."

"I love you." The rogue words roll off my tongue, never bothering to check with my brain before leaping into existence. Elijah stiffens in my arms for a second, even his breath stilling. My heart gallops in my chest, waiting for his response, but wholly unprepared at the same time.

But the seconds tick by, and he doesn't say anything. I glance down at him to find his eyes closed, but there's too much tension in his face for him to truly be asleep. Maybe I should be grateful for his avoidance. Maybe we can pretend this didn't happen and find our way back to casual. Something tells me it can't possibly be that easy though. There's no way back from here, not without broken hearts.

Eventually, his body relaxes against mine, his breathing growing deep and even as he falls into sleep. I lay awake and count the ceiling tiles until the sun starts to come up, only then do my heavy eyelids finally fall closed for a few hours of fitful sleep.

CHAPTER 27

Elijah

Time is an illusion. According to quantum physics it's a relative concept. And I can now confirm that it absolutely ceases to exist when you're mired in doubt about a relationship, watching your phone for any form of contact from the other person.

I haven't heard from Pax since we got back from Wisconsin last weekend. He said he had off work until after the new year. Stupidly, I thought that might mean he'd want to hang out more, but I've spent the past week alone in my apartment with hardly a single text, driving myself crazy replaying that pivotal moment in my mind where it all went wrong.

I love you.

The words echo in my mind over and over, followed by the deafening silence I gave him in reply. The problem is, I don't even know if he's avoiding me because he said those words or because I *didn't* say them. I pretended to be asleep, and then I snuck out of bed as soon as the sun came up. I don't blame Pax for not wanting to talk to me after that.

Theo would know what to do, but I can't call him about this. If I'd told him about this thing with Pax from the start maybe it would be fine, but now there would be too many questions, too much to explain. And considering it's starting to feel like whatever it was between us is over, it would be unnecessary angst to tell Theo about it now.

There's only one other person who might have some insight, so I pick up my phone and make the call.

"Hey!" Alex answers enthusiastically.

"Hey," I say. "How, um, how've your holidays been?"

"Ugh, I'm ready to get back to school."

I find myself relaxing, a small smile forming on my lips. "I can relate."

"So, what's up? You must have called for a reason, right? I mean, who makes phone calls anymore?" There's a light teasing in his voice.

"I'm sorry, should I not have called?" My stomach squirms, and I bite my bottom lip. This is why making friends is so hard—there are always rules I don't know about.

"I was kidding; you can totally call. I was only curious if there was a reason or if you just missed me like crazy and absolutely *had* to hear my voice."

I chuckle, some of the tension easing out of my stomach. "I kind of need advice."

"About that sexy man of yours?" he

281

guesses.

"Yeah."

"I'm listening."

"Okay." I take a deep breath, trying to think of where exactly to start. "I spent Christmas with his family and things have been weird since then. Actually, things were weird for about two weeks before that."

"Define weird," he prompts.

"He's hardly been texting me; we used to text every day. And for a little while there it was like he wanted to see me as much as possible, now he's avoiding me like the plague. God, saying it out loud it's so obvious. He's bored with me, right? We weren't dating so there's no breakup—it's just *over*."

"Maybe, but hold on, I feel like I'm missing something. Did anything else happen or he just all the sudden started being the Ice Man?"

"On Christmas he kind of, um, well, he said he loved me," I confess.

"Way to bury the lead on that one," Alex grumbles. "And you said it back, then what happened?"

"No, I didn't," I correct.

"What?"

"It was *right* after...*you know*. I wasn't sure if it was a chemical reaction in his brain or a test or what. And it caught me off guard. I didn't know what to say."

"All right, we can fix this," he assures me.

The sound of my door buzzer startles me into nearly dropping my phone. My heart jumps into my throat as I set my book down and hop off the couch to hit the button, knowing it can only be Pax.

"Oh my god, I think he's here."

"Pax?" Alex asks.

"Yeah, I can't think of who else would show up unannounced."

"Okay, listen, he's probably feeling vulnerable, so he's either going to act like nothing ever happened and try to fuck you to prove to both of you that nothing has changed," he advises.

"Or?" I prompt.

"Or, he's going to try to break things off."

"What do I do if it's the second option?" We said this was casual way back when it first started, but it doesn't feel so casual anymore. It makes sense that Pax would pull back. I broke the rules. We both did.

"Do you want to be with him?" Alex asks.

"Yeah."

"Are you in love with him?"

I swallow around the lump in my throat and nod my head, realizing a second later that Alex can't see me. "Y-yeah."

"Then don't let him go. Tell him how you feel. He feels vulnerable, so you need to even the playing field and make yourself vulnerable too."

"You think that'll work?" I ask, clutching my phone harder. The buzzer sounds again, and I finally cross the room to press the button to let him in.

"I don't know, but it's the best advice I have."

"Ugh, this is so much more complicated than rocket science," I groan.

"Tell me about it," he chuckles.

"Okay, wish me luck."

"Good luck," Alex says, and then we both hang up.

I put my phone away and smooth my hands over my shirt as I listen for the sound of his heavy footfalls coming up the stairs, my stomach twisting itself in knots. When he comes into view at the top of the staircase, his shoulders are more slumped than usual, his expression uncharacteristically tight.

"Pax, is everything okay?" I ask, stepping aside to let him in. Is that why he hasn't been texting all week? Did something happen? Or was Alex right? Is this all about him feeling too vulnerable?

"Hey, Einstein," he greets me with a weak smile, pulling me in for a hug as soon as he reaches me. "I know I showed up unannounced, but do you mind if I come in for a few minutes?"

"Of course." I step aside to let him in. "Is everything okay?" I ask again since he didn't answer the first time.

"Yeah, I just wanted to talk."

My stomach sinks. That doesn't sound

great. Not that I have a lot of relationship experience, *obviously*, but I'm pretty sure "we have to talk" is never good.

"Um...yeah...of course." I wave him over to the couch, gathering up my mess of notes and putting them on the coffee table so he'll have somewhere to sit.

Pax

My stomach twists, and my heart hammers against my ribs as I watch Elijah scurry around, clearing a space for me to sit and then rushing off to the kitchen to get me a drink I didn't ask for. He tugs at the hem of his shirt and runs his hands through his hair, as twitchy and nervous as a rabbit. A damn adorable rabbit that I can't stop wanting to touch and kiss and fucking *be* with. But I have to.

He tries to move past me again; I didn't even hear whatever the excuse was this time, what he claimed to need from somewhere else in the shoebox sized apartment. I snag his bicep as he tries to pass, giving myself one last second to appreciate the heat of his skin, the smoothness of it under my fingertips. I look down into his eyes as he uses his free hand to push his glasses up his nose.

"I'm not boyfriend material, Einstein," I confess.

"What do you mean?" he asks, looking up at me with a soft, innocent expression.

"I mean," I sigh, running my free hand through my hair. "I'm gone *all* the time for work. I had this boyfriend a couple of years ago. He was a great guy, and I liked him a lot. He was always telling me how much it sucked that I traveled so much, and I kept promising that I'd get a promotion soon and wouldn't have to travel anymore. But the thing was, I didn't want that promotion, and I didn't want to be stuck in the same office Monday through Friday. I *like* that I travel most weeks."

Elijah shrugs. "I don't mind if you travel. Honestly, it's kind of perfect for me. Not that I don't like having you around, but I also really like my own space and time to myself."

My heart fills with hope, but I'm afraid to believe in it. "I cheat," I tack on what I'm sure will be the nail in the coffin of this whole idea of a proper relationship. "I'm not proud of it, and I know it makes me the scummiest guy alive, but I cheated on more than one boyfriend before I gave up and accepted the fact that I'm *not boyfriend material*." I stress the last three words again, hoping he'll get it, hoping he'll agree with me and tell me to leave before we both get hurt. But also hoping he won't. "I don't want to hurt you, Nerdlet. I'd never forgive myself."

He studies me for several long moments, his expression not giving anything away.

"Do you want to be with other people?" he finally asks.

My heart stutters at the thought, my entire body recoiling at the very idea of it. Of course I don't want anyone else.

"No," I answer easily.

"Okay, well if that changes, talk to me about it, and we'll figure it out. You can't cheat if I don't have any expectations," he reasons.

"But that's the thing." I cup his face between my hands, my heart beating so hard I'm sure it's going to burst out of my chest. "I *want* you to have expectations. You *deserve* to have expectations."

"I deserve to be with the person I want to be with," he counters. "I'm sorry I didn't say it on Christmas, but I was scared and a little confused. But I love you, Paxton Reynolds. I don't want anyone else. I haven't even *noticed* anyone else in my entire life. I want to be with you, and if that means making compromises about other people in the future, or missing you during the week, or whatever other excuse you're going to throw at me, I don't care. iIt's all worth it if it means I can be with you."

"Elijah," I breathe out his name like a prayer, losing the will to argue. I want this more than I've ever wanted anything, even in the face of all the fear.

His gaze holds mine, full of the confidence I knew was inside him all along. My chest warms all the way through to my soul knowing that *I* helped him find that confidence. And then, just like that first night at Alex's party, he doesn't give me a choice. He loops his arms around my neck and presses his lips to mine. I thread my fingers through his hair and pull him fully against me, ready for the first time for the explosion we create.

I drag my teeth along his bottom lip and then slip my tongue into his mouth, kissing him deep and long, this time not shying away from the feeling that expands in my chest, warm and fuzzy and too big to be contained inside me.

"I fucking love the hell out of you, Einstein."

"Does that mean we've upgraded from casual?" he asks with a grin, his nose brushing against mine, his warm breath fanning over my damp lips.

"We've upgraded," I agree. "We've got the premium package now, which includes overnight stays and all kinds of expectations."

"I can live with that," he agrees. "Will you stay the night tonight?"

"Try to get me to leave." I smirk, and he laughs, his chest vibrating against mine as I hold him tighter.

"So...do you want to go to bed?" he asks slyly.

"You read my mind, Nerdlet."

CHAPTER 28

Elijah

I startle awake from a dream about being buried alive. The reason for the dream is immediately clear when I realize there's a mountain of sweaty, heavy man on top of me. Not just any man, my *boyfriend*. I smile, even as I struggle to roll the mountain of snoring human flesh off of me. *I'm waking up next to my boyfriend.*

I manage to slip out from underneath him, grabbing my underwear off the floor where they ended up once we got into bed last night. I smile at the memory, a slight ache still in my backside as a souvenir. Pulling them on, I make my way to the bathroom to pee and brush my teeth. I know Pax doesn't think I wake up minty fresh, but this is a new relationship; we can keep some magic in it for a little while. Once I'm clean and smelling nice, I climb back into bed and wiggle into his arms again.

"Mmph," he mumbles. "Don't get up."

"I'm not. I'm getting *back* into bed," I assure him.

"Good, stay." He tightens his arms around me and pulls me against him, pressing his face into the crook of my neck and inhaling deeply.

We lay like that for a while, half awake, half asleep, trading lazy kisses every so often as the sun rises higher outside the window.

My stomach growls eventually, and Pax finally opens his eyes fully.

"I guess I'd better feed you. Sorry, I'm pretty rusty at this boyfriend thing. You'll have to remind me if you need regular walks or anything."

I chuckle and bite his shoulder playfully.

"I'm fully capable of feeding myself, so you can cross that off your list of boyfriend duties. I was just too comfortable in bed with you to bother with breakfast."

"That's understandable," he agrees with a yawn. "Why don't we go out for breakfast?"

"Sounds good, but five more minutes of cuddling first," I negotiate, and Pax laughs.

"Five more minutes," he agrees.

It's well past breakfast by the time we drag ourselves out of bed.

"How about a shower?" Pax suggests.

"What? Together?"

"Yes, together," he says with a smirk. "It's a very *boyfriend* thing to do." The way he purrs the word makes me wonder if he likes it as much as I do. I know he said he loves me, but it's hard to believe it's really true, that after all the years of wanting and everything that's happened that he really wants me as much as I want him. How long will he feel this way? What if he gets sick of me in a week or a month? My heart climbs into my throat, making it hard to breathe. How do people do this? All the uncertainty that comes along with relationships is excruciating.

Pax rounds the bed and drops a kiss against my lips. "Don't overthink it, Nerdlet. This is all good; let's enjoy it."

"Yeah," I agree, smiling up at him. "But my shower's pretty small."

"That's half the fun," he assures me with a wink.

I slide my underwear down and toss them into my hamper and then follow Pax into the bathroom. He already has the shower running, and I eye the small space, more than certain that we're not both going to fit comfortably, but if Pax wants to try, I'm always up for an interesting experiment. Particularly the kind of experiment that has Pax and I naked together.

Once the water's warm, we step inside, water immediately hitting me square in the face as we both try to maneuver our way in.

"Shit," he mutters, reaching up to adjust the shower head while I shove my head under his arm to keep from being drowned. "That's better," he declares, and I peek my head out to find out. I'm no longer being waterboarded, so that's an improvement, but Pax is pressed up against one wall while I'm squished against the other, our bodies flush against each other.

"Told you it was small."

"And I told *you* that was half the fun," he says, looking down at me with a grin before reaching for my bottle of body wash on the shelf. He pours some into his hands and then rubs them together to lather them up. "See, now I get to put my hands all over you with the excuse of washing you."

"Ah, yes, I can see the genius in this plan."

Pax takes his time washing me *thoroughly*, making sure every inch of me is spotless, particularly between my butt cheeks.

"Stop teasing," I complain, pressing my hardening cock against his thigh.

"Not my fault you're insatiable," he replies demurely.

"*I'm* insatiable?" I scoff. "I seem to remember *someone* waking me up twice in the middle of the night, grinding his thick, hard erection against me," I remind him, dropping my voice low and running my hands over his chest and down his stomach.

"Now who's teasing?" he points out.

"Both of us, I guess."

Washing each other turns into hurried, slippery hand-jobs before we make it out of the shower and manage to get dressed.

"There's a little diner down the street that serves breakfast all day—want to walk there?" he suggests.

"Anywhere with food sounds good to me,"

I assure him.

Pax laces his fingers through mine as we step out onto the sidewalk, the January morning cool, even in California. The gesture is so simple, but it feels like it speaks volumes. He's not trying to hide us, even in front of strangers who may be homophobic assholes.

"What?" he asks, noticing my gaze on our linked hands.

"Nothing." I shrug, letting my happiness shine through my smile. Pax grins and tugs me forward for another kiss. I'm starting to think he likes kissing me just as much as I like kissing him. Butterflies invade my stomach, and my heart trips over its own beats as I kiss him back, basking in the pure happiness of simply *being* with him.

"I love you, Pax."

"I love you," he murmurs back against my lips.

My stomach growls again, and we both laugh. "Come on, let's get you food before you start gnawing on my arm."

Pax

The waitress at the diner doesn't even blink when we order coffee and breakfast food, even though it's well into the afternoon.

"Can I ask you a question?" Elijah asks once our order is placed and the waitress is gone.

"Considering your last question was

about rimming, I can assure you, my interest is piqued," I tease.

He blushes and flicks the wadded up paper from his straw at me from across the table. "It's not that kind of question."

"Okay, shoot, Einstein."

"I'm wondering what the rules are now. I've never had a boyfriend, and I don't want to mess this up by doing something stupid."

I let out a humorless laugh and slide my foot against his under the table. "I'm no expert either, Nerdlet. I think I made that pretty clear last night when I told you how bad I am at relationships."

"If neither of us knows the rules, that means we make the rules, right?"

"I guess it does," I agree.

"So, what are the rules?" he asks again, and I laugh.

"Communication. That sounds very mature, right?" I suggest. "If there's a problem, we talk about it."

He nods. "I like that. And the same for if you, um, want someone else."

"I don't want anyone else," I say vehemently, even if there's a small voice in the back of my head that points out that I have a shitty track record of staying faithful.

"But *if*."

"Okay, yes, but it's not going to happen," I insist.

"What else? Sleepovers are allowed now, right?" he asks.

"Sleepovers are encouraged," I agree, and he smiles.

"Good, I like sleepovers."

"Me too," I agree. "I think that's enough rules, we can figure things out as we go."

"And if I do something stupid or if you get freaked out again?" Elijah asks, tugging his bottom lip between his teeth.

"Then rule one applies, we talk about it; we work it out like adults and shit."

"And shit," he mocks, and I wad up my napkin to throw at him. He dodges it and sticks his tongue out.

"I seriously fucking love you, Nerdlet. That's the only thing that matters; we'll figure the rest out."

"Okay," he agrees. "We'll figure the rest out."

CHAPTER 29

Elijah

My stomach flutters when I see Theo's name flash across my phone screen. I've been avoiding his calls since Pax and I made things official because now that it's real, I know I have to tell him.

I hover my finger over the green *accept* button, willing myself to be brave and push it, just tell him the truth and get it over with. *He won't be mad,* I lie to myself.

"You can do it," I say with determination, mashing my finger against the screen of my phone to answer the call. "Hello?"

"Dude, what the hell?"

"What?" I cringe at myself.

"Don't what me, asshole. You've been dodging me for almost two weeks. What gives?"

I sigh, getting up from the table and going over to the couch to get comfortable for what I'm sure will be a sucky conversation.

"There's something I have to tell you that I've been trying to work up the nerve to say," I admit, pulling my knees up and resting my arms on them.

"E, you're my best friend in the world; there's nothing you could say that would change that. Tell me."

"Okay." I take a deep breath and hold it for a second before slowly letting it out. "The guy I told you about, the one I was...*you know* with."

"Yeah?" he says, his voice sounding tight.

"It was Pax," I confess, bracing myself for anger, disappointment, disgust. Instead, I'm met with a long silence from Theo's end of the phone.

I pull the phone away from my ear to make sure we're still connected, and then bite down on my bottom lip to give myself something to do while Theo processes the information or finishes formulating a lecture, I'm not sure which.

"I know," he says after two hundred heartbeats.

"You...you *know*?" I repeat. "How?"

"I saw the way he was looking at you at Christmas. I asked him about it, and he confessed."

"Why didn't you say anything?" I ask.

"Why didn't you?" he throws back at me, the accusation in his tone hitting me square in the chest.

"Because you were so mad at the guy when I told you about the first encounter, I was afraid if you knew it was Pax, you would hate him."

There's another long pause before he responds. "That's fair. I *do* hate him a little."

"Please don't hate him. I won't be able to

live with myself if I cause a rift between the two of you."

"He's my brother; I'll get over it eventually," Theo assures me. "But why are you telling me all this now? Did you two break things off?"

"No, the opposite actually," I confess. "We made things official, I guess?"

He huffs out a laugh. "You guess? Is he your boyfriend or not?"

"Yeah, he's my boyfriend." Saying the word makes my stomach flutter, a smile tilting my lips. "God, I never thought I'd say that. I have a *boyfriend*."

"I'm glad, E. I mean that," he says. "I'm still mad at Pax for stringing you along for months, but you sound really happy and that makes me happy."

"I *am* happy," I tell him honestly. "I...god, this is embarrassing to say, but I've had a crush on Pax forever. I never thought he'd see me the same way."

"That explains it, then," he says with a hint of sadness.

"Explains what?"

"Why you never looked twice at me." He laughs, but it sounds hollow.

"What?" I press the phone harder to my ear, my heart beating faster. "What do you mean?"

"Nothing, it's stupid." There's a sort of forced cheerfulness in his voice now. "I want you to have the happiest life anyone has ever had, I mean that."

"Thanks, T. You know I love you, right?"

"I love you too," he replies, another dip of sorrow in his tone. "I've gotta go, but while I have you, I wanted to let you know I *am* going to be moving out to Cali, so you'll be seeing me again before you know it."

"You are? That's so great."

"Yeah. I have to study for a test, so I'll talk to you later, okay? And tell Pax I love him too."

"I will," I promise.

We hang up, and I feel lighter now that this secret is no longer hanging between us, but it also feels like something vital has shifted in our relationship, and I have no idea what it is.

Unfolding my legs, I spread myself out on the couch and type out a text to Pax.

Elijah: I talked to Theo, told him we're dating. He took it well...probably because he already knew about us. Know anything about that?

Pax: I MAY have told him over Christmas

Elijah: Thanks for the heads up, so glad I wasn't lying awake at night worrying about that for the past several weeks

Pax: Sorry, don't be mad

Elijah: I'm not mad. I'm glad it's not hanging over my head anymore. It makes things between us feel more real

Pax: I'll show you real as soon as I get home tomorrow ;)
Elijah: Looking forward to it

I type another message but hesitate to send it for a few seconds before hitting the button.

Elijah: I love you
Pax: I love you to the moon and back
Elijah: That's far!
Pax: I KNOW
Pax: Gotta go, client just walked in

I read the words several times, a goofy smile on my face, before finally closing the text thread and getting back to studying.

Pax

I stride out of the meeting feeling like I'm king of the fucking world. I type out a text to Elijah telling him I closed the deal and then shove my phone back into my pocket and hail a taxi to take me back to the hotel.

Normally after I close a deal this big, I go out to celebrate. Before Elijah, that celebration tended to include a willing man in my bed. That's what got me into trouble with other boyfriends before I decided I wasn't a relationship kind of guy. The crazy thing is, the absolute last thing I want is someone other than Elijah.

Back in my hotel room, I drop my brief-case near the foot of the bed and shoot off a quick email to my boss to let him know I sealed the deal. I'm full of too much excited energy to sit down, so I decide to head down to the hotel bar for a celebratory drink.

I slide onto one of the stools at the bar top and flag down the bartender to order a scotch, neat.

Taking a sip of my drink, I swivel in my seat to people watch a bit, letting the peace of a job well done and the end of another week settle over me. I reach into my pocket and type out a quick text to my brother.

Pax: We cool?
Theo: Same deal still stands, hurt him and I'll kill you. But yeah, we're cool
Pax: I love him
Theo: I know

"This seat taken?" a voice asks, pulling my attention away from my phone. I look up to see a handsome man pointing at the open stool be-side me. The bar is less than half-full, there are at least a dozen places he could sit; he's not asking about the seat.

I look him up and down, his suit nicely fitted, a confident grin on his full lips. I have no doubt he'd be a fun time. Even after our initial conversation where we put everything out there and agreed to make things official, Elijah has insisted that he doesn't have any expectations and thus I *can't* cheat on him. But I don't want anyone else. Maybe I wasn't mature enough with my other relationships, maybe it *is* the lack of pressure from Elijah, or maybe it's just Elijah himself. But the next word out of my mouth is the easiest one I've ever spoken.

"Sorry." I shake my head and give him an apologetic smile.

"No problem." He tilts his head in understanding and claims a stool at the other end of the bar.

I pull my phone back out and re-open the text thread to Theo.

Pax: I'm pretty sure he's The One. You know, marriage, a bunch of dogs, all that shit
Theo: You're planning to propose?!!
Pax: Relax lol, not anytime soon, but one day maybe
Theo: Be good to him
Pax: I promise

CHAPTER 30

Pax

The trudge up the steps to my apartment after a long week away is as tiresome as it always is. My flight was delayed by several hours this afternoon, so it's already after ten, which means my chances of catching Elijah are probably slim. Unless, of course, he's waiting up to hear from me. The thought causes a smile to spread across my face and I pick up my pace, taking the steps two at a time. Maybe if I call him, I can convince him to come over and spend the weekend in bed with me. We can live off takeout and orgasm until Monday rolls back around and forces me to leave again.

As thrilling as the idea is, it twists the knife in my gut as well, a reminder that he may say he's fine with my work schedule, but eventually he'll be sick of it. He'll want more of my time and attention; he'll want me to be home on weeknights.

As I make my way down the hall to my apartment, the smell of something delicious tickles my nose and makes my stomach rumble, reminding me I haven't eaten since breakfast. Reaching into my pocket, I snag my keys and unlock my door. The mouthwatering smell gets stronger, the sound of dishes clanging together echoing from my kitchen.

"Hello?" I call out cautiously. I doubt someone broke into my place to cook dinner, but you never know.

"Pax?" Elijah's voice calls out, and the smile I was wearing previously is back in full force, the twisting in my gut replaced by a whole herd of crack addled butterflies.

I drop my briefcase and leave my suitcase by the door, striding down the hall with purpose toward the kitchen. I pause in the doorway, taking in the sight of him standing at the stove in a pair of sweatpants that are entirely too big on him, hanging low on his hips, and a shirt that's just as miss sized. He looks over his shoulder at me, a shy smile appearing as quickly as the sweet blush does.

"I hope you don't mind I came over when you weren't here. You gave me that spare key, and I figured since your flight was delayed you might be hungry and maybe too tired to make dinner by the time you got home. If it's weird, I can go, and I promise I won't do it again, I ju—" I close the distance between us in a flash, spinning him around and trapping him against the counter as I drag my fingers through his thick, curly hair, tilt his face up, and kiss the hell out of him.

He melts against me, reaching for the front

of my shirt and holding on tight as he kisses me back. Every stress I had this week, every doubt about whether we can make this work, all melt away. We can make this work, because I won't allow it to be any other way. Elijah is mine, now and forever.

"I take it that means you don't mind me being here when you got home?" he asks when the kiss ends. I huff out a laugh, resting my forehead against his.

There are a million answers I could give. I could tell him I love that he's here, that it saved me the trouble of calling and convincing him to come over, that I've missed him all week. But my mouth makes a decision before my brain can catch up.

"You should move in with me."

"What?" He laughs nervously.

"Move in with me," I say again, this time my brain has caught up and is fully on board with the decision my mouth made. "I want you here every week when I get home. I want to share every inch of my life with you."

"Isn't it a little fast?" He bites his bottom lip, twisting his fingers tighter around the fabric of my shirt.

"It doesn't feel too fast for me. Does it feel too fast to you?"

"No, I guess not." He loosens his grip, and his nervous expression turns into a shy smile. He drags in a deep breath and then nods. "Okay, I'll move in, as long as you're sure."

"I've never been more sure of anything in my life."

And then I kiss him again because he's mine and I can.

The sound of the oven timer is the only thing that keeps me from picking him up, carrying him to my bed, and enacting my plan of keeping him there all weekend. He pulls away and checks what appears to be a casserole in the oven.

"It probably won't be very good, but I got this recipe from your mom. She said it's your favorite."

"You did?" If I wasn't already in love with him, I think I'd fall right now. He tugs at the hem of the overly large shirt he's wearing and shrugs like it's no big deal.

"I wanted to do something nice for you; I know you had a long week."

"I love you," I tell him because there's never been anything more true.

"I love you," he says simply, and I wonder if it's possible for a heart to actually burst with happiness.

"Are you wearing my clothes?" I ask, putting the pieces together for the first time. He blushes bright red again as he pulls dinner out of the oven and places it on top of the stove to cool.

"There was a bit of a mishap with the flour when I was making the biscuits for the top," he explains. "I hope you don't mind?"

"I fucking love it. We should have a new rule once you live here: you can only wear my clothes or be absolutely naked when we're home together."

He chuckles. "You may be able to convince me to agree to that."

"Oh yeah? How about we start negotiations after dinner then?" I suggest.

"Okay, but I'll warn you, I drive a *hard* bargain," he teases with a grin.

"Oh my god, Einstein, did you just make a dirty pun?" I bark out a laugh. "I didn't think it was possible, but I'm more in love with you right now than I was thirty seconds ago."

"Hopefully this isn't a bell curve situation."

"Not a chance, Nerdlet, not a chance."

Elijah

Unfortunately, after dinner we don't get the chance to have any sort of *negotiations*. Pax gets a text from his friends, and the next thing I know, I'm being dragged out of the house—still wearing Pax's overly large clothes, by the way—to go be social at a bar. When I told him anything he could throw at me would be worth it if it meant getting to be with him, I did *not* mean being social on a moment's notice.

"Come on, Einstein, we're celebrating our impending cohabitation—put on a smile," Pax urges as we pull into the bar parking lot.

"I look silly; I'm wearing your clothes."

"You look like you're *mine*," he purrs, leaning over the center console to press a hungry kiss to my lips. "It's hot as fuck," he murmurs as he licks the seam of my lips and then slips his tongue into my mouth.

My cock throbs, and I moan into his mouth, reaching for the front of his shirt to keep him from getting away.

"Come on, just a few hours, and then I promise I'll make it up to you when we get *home*." The way he says the last word sends a happy shiver through me. We still have to go through all the headache of breaking my lease and moving my stuff, but we're going to live *together*. This is for real.

"Okay, but don't let anyone laugh at my clothes," I say.

"I promise," he assures me, pressing one last kiss to my lips before pulling back and getting out of the car.

He slips his hand into mine as we walk into the, bar and I smile up at him in surprise.

"You're better at this boyfriend thing than you think you are," I tell him, pressing my palm against his and squeezing our fingers together.

We spot his friends at a table in the corner and make our way over to them.

"Well don't you two look simply domestic," Hudson teases, smirking at our joined hands as soon as we get close. "And are you wearing Pax's clothes?"

I shrink against my boyfriend, heat rising in my cheeks.

"That shade of green looks terrible on you, man," Pax scolds his friend. "Jealousy is not becoming. If you want a sweet little boyfriend of your own, you've got one waiting for you right across the table. So, either stop jerking him around or shut the fuck up."

Bishop blushes even worse than me, and Seph tries to hide her snicker with a cough. Hudson scowls but doesn't say another word.

"We didn't think you'd actually show. We figured you'd be too *busy*," Seph says, waggling her eyebrows at us.

"We had some news we wanted to celebrate, so your text came at the perfect time," Pax says.

Bishop makes a strangled, excited sound. "Oh my god, did you guys get engaged?"

"Whoa, no, we've only been officially dating a few weeks; we're not rushing down the aisle," Pax assures him. "But we *are* moving in together."

"Oh my gosh, that's so exciting," Seph squeals, clapping her hands together.

"Fair warning, Pax leaves dirty underwear all over the place, and he always leaves the bathroom a mess," Hudson advises.

"That was back in college," Pax says, roll-

K.M. Neuhold

ing his eyes.

"I don't care if he's messy," I say, looking up at Pax with a smile.

"You guys are gross," Hudson complains.

"I think it's sweet," Bishop counters.

"I need another drink," Hudson says, hopping off his stool and heading over to the bar.

Pax joins him, getting us a couple of drinks and then returning to the table.

"Apparently Hudson found someone more interesting than his friends," Bishop says when Hudson chooses to crash a table full of cute guys rather than return to sit with us. I reach across the table and pat his hand. The gesture feels a little awkward, but when he smiles at me, I know it was the right thing to do.

Seph talks my ear off about decorating Pax's place so it will feel like *ours* instead of his, while Bishop chats with Pax and seems to do his best not to look at Hudson every few seconds. Eventually, Bishop gets up to get himself another drink. I watch as the bartender leans over the bar a little, smiling at him.

"Is he flirting?" I ask Pax, nodding my head toward the two of them. He follows my gaze and chuckles.

"Yup. It can be tricky to tell with someone angling for tips, but his body language is definitely giving him away he wants more than a *tip* from our friend Bishop."

Bishop seems to soak up the attention,

blushing and grinning back at the tattooed, muscular bartender. When he gets his drink, he looks back over in our direction with a question in his eyes. Pax waves him away, and Bishop smiles again, claiming a seat at the bar instead of coming back over to sit with us.

We stay and chat with Seph a little longer before Pax declares it time to go home and get some *sleep*. Yes, he says it so suggestively I swear my face has to be as red as a tomato as Seph laughs and tells us to have fun.

We stop by the bar to say goodbye to Bishop before we go.

"You good, man?" Pax checks.

Bishop glances over at the bartender who's currently serving another customer, but who's barely left his side since he sat down over an hour ago.

"Yeah, Riot seems really nice. I'm going to hang out until his shift ends."

"All right, be safe." Pax claps his friend on the shoulder and then waves at Hudson from across the bar as we head out.

"He's going to have sex with the bartender even though he's in love with Hudson?" I ask once we're outside.

"Sometimes relationships are complicated, Nerdlet."

"You're telling me," I huff out a chuckle. "I still think rocket science makes a lot more sense than all this." I wave between us and Pax smiles.

"Maybe, but our explosions are more fun," he jokes, sweeping me up into his arms.

"I'm not sure about that," I tease. "Take me home and let's find out."

EPILOGUE

Four Years Later
Elijah

"I think this is the last one; where does it go?" Pax asks, coming into the kitchen with a box in his arms, his muscles straining the sleeves of his t-shirt, the tattoos on his arms glistening from exertion. I lick my lips, my cock growing hard as I mentally undress him. "Einstein, my eyes are up here," he teases, and I flick my gaze to his face with a grin.

"Sorry, but there are other parts of you that are a *lot* more interesting than your eyes."

"Is that so? Am I nothing but a piece of meat to you?" he jokes, and I shrug with a smirk.

He lets the box fall from his arms, hitting the floor with a thud.

"Hey, there could've been something fragile in there," I complain, rounding the counter of our brand-new kitchen to see what exactly might've been damaged. But before I can open the box, Pax's arms come around my waist, and he lifts me onto the counter. His lips press against mine, my legs going instantly around his waist.

I kiss him back hungrily, running my hands through his hair, tugging at it just a little as I meet his tongue with my own, giving as good as I get. His hands wander over my hips until they make their way to the front of my jeans, unzipping my pants with the kind of ease and familiarity that comes with four years of bliss. Okay, maybe it hasn't *all* been bliss. Hudson was one hundred percent right about Pax's slobbish ways and yes, they absolutely drive me crazy. But, mostly bliss.

It took him about a year to lose his fear that he might cheat or that I might get sick of his work schedule. I was never worried about either, not really.

His mouth is hot against mine, his lips salty from sweat after hauling boxes all morning. I reach between us and open his pants too, pulling his thick, hard cock out of his underwear and stroking it in my hand a few times. He grunts into my mouth, his tongue tangling with mine, before he bats my hand away and takes over.

His large hand encircles both our shafts. I moan, letting my head fall back, my fingers digging into Pax's shoulders as he jerks us off together. Our precum mixes, slicking the way for his fist as he strokes us, rotating his right every time he reaches our heads.

"Oh god, just like that," I moan.

He kisses along my throat, nipping and licking at my skin. His balls bounce against mine with every jerk of our cocks.

I tighten my legs around his waist, thrusting into his fist, our moans filling the kitchen and echoing off the walls. For the first time ever, we're not in an apartment so we don't have to worry about being quiet for neighbors. Not that we were ever particularly quiet, but now we don't have to *worry*.

"Fuck," he groans, his cock pulsing against mine, thick, milky cum spilling over my erection as he continues to jerk us. That's all it takes to send me over the edge, my balls tightening so hard I can hardly breathe, my orgasm thundering through me as my release joins his in covering both of us.

He works his hand over us until we're both over-sensitive and starting to soften.

"Are you sure you're happy?" I ask the question that's been on my mind since I took the job with NASA that required us to move from California to Texas.

Pax glances down at our cum soaked skin, our softening cocks still hanging out obscenely, and he chuckles. "Yeah, I'm pretty happy, Nerdlet."

"Not about the sex." I push his shoulder and roll my eyes. "I mean with our lives. You're sure you're okay living in Texas and taking this promotion that's going to keep you in the office instead of traveling?"

"I'm a little nervous about being in the

same office day in and day out, but I think I'm ready to put the traveling behind me and be home with you during the week. Besides, I think Winston and Leo will be much happier to have me around more," he points out, and on cue our two snorty, smelly pugs come trotting into the kitchen.

"I'll be glad to have you around more too. I just want to make sure it's what you want."

"Einstein, listen to me." He cups my jaw in his hand and holds my gaze. "You are the absolute love of my life. If we needed to move to the moon for you to do your crazy scientist shit, then that's what we'd do."

"We're a *least* a decade from having a NASA branch stationed on the moon," I assure him.

"At least the boxes will weigh less when we move there," he counters.

"I love you too, by the way." I lean in and kiss his lips again, still giddy after four years at the fact that I *can*, that he's all mine to kiss him all I want.

"I know," he says solemnly, ruining it with that shit-eating grin of his. I shove his shoulder again and when he steps back, I slide off the counter and tuck myself into my jeans, zipping them back up.

"Oh, there's just one more thing, Nerdlet," he says, stepping back and making himself decent as well. Then, he reaches into his pocket and drops to one knee.

"What's happening?"

"Shh, I'm trying to do something here," he scolds. He holds a small box out, flipping the lid open in a fluid motion to display a dark silver ring. "I've been thinking about this whole speech for weeks now and to be honest, I'm not sure how to fit everything you make me feel into a few sentences. You're the smartest, sexiest, most incredible man I've ever known, and I'm hoping like hell you'll agree to let me spend the rest of my life in awe of the fact that you actually chose me."

I cover my mouth with my hands to hide the unattractive gaping thing my mouth is doing without my permission. "What is happening?" I ask again, my brain unable to process the moment.

"I'm proposing," he explains with a laugh. "Say yes?"

"Oh my god, are you kidding?" I gasp. "Yes, of course. Come back up here before I faint." I wave him up off his knees and take the ring he hands to me.

"It's made from a meteorite; I thought you'd like it."

"It's amazing." I run my index finger over the smooth metal in wonder before looking at Pax again. "This is the complete opposite of casual," I point out.

"I'm aware. I figured we moved past casual a while ago—the time seemed right to take the big step."

"You think we're ready?" I ask, stepping into his arms and resting my head against his chest.

"What's to be ready for?" Pax counters. "It's marriage, not rocket science."

The End

MORE BY K.M.NEUHOLD

Stand Alones
Change of Heart

Heathens Ink
Rescue Me
Going Commando
From Ashes
Shattered Pieces
Inked in Vegas
Flash Me

Inked (AKA Heathens Ink Spin-off stories)
Unraveled
Uncomplicated

Replay
Face the Music
Play it by Ear
Beat of Their Own Drum
Strike a Chord

Ballsy Boys
Rebel

K.M. Neuhold

Tank
Heart
Campy
Pixie
Don't Miss The Kinky Boys Coming Soon

Working Out The Kinks
Stay
Heel

Short Stand Alones
That One Summer (YA)
Always You
Kiss and Run (Valentine's Inc Book 4)

ABOUT THE AUTHOR

Author K.M.Neuhold is a complete romance junkie, a total sap in every way. She started her journey as an author in new adult, MF romance, but after a chance reading of an MM book she was completely hooked on everything about lovely- and sometimes damaged- men finding their Happily Ever After together. She has a strong passion for writing characters with a lot of heart and soul, and a bit of humor as well. And she fully admits that her OCD tendencies of making sure every side character has a full backstory will likely always lead to every book having a spin-off or series. When she's not writing she's a lion tamer, an astronaut, and a superhero...just kidding, she's likely watching Netflix and snuggling with her husky while her amazing husband brings her coffee.

STALK ME

Website: authorkmneuhold.com
Email: kmneuhold@gmail.com
Instagram: @KMNeuhold
Twitter: @KMNeuhold
Bookbub
Join my Mailing List for special bonus scenes and teasers!
Facebook reader group- Neuhold's Nerds You want to be here, we have crazy amounts of fun